Dead Glamorous

Dead Glamorous

*The Autobiography of
Seduction and
Self-Destruction*

Carole Morin

VICTOR GOLLANCZ

LONDON

First published in Great Britain 1996
by Victor Gollancz
An imprint of the Cassell Group
Wellington House, 125 Strand, London WC2R 0BB

A catalogue record for this book is
available from the British Library.

ISBN 0 575 06172 3

Typeset by Rowland Phototypesetting Ltd,
Bury St Edmunds, Suffolk
Printed and bound in Great Britain by
St Edmundsbury Press Ltd,
Bury St Edmunds, Suffolk
96 97 98 99   10 9 8 7 6 5 4 3 2 1

For Dangerous Donald, a thrill a minute and he has blue eyes.

Contents

John died today. He's my brother. He committed suicide. Of course he didn't die today. He died on this date, six years ago. Deaths are easier to remember than birthdays.

Today is always as good a day as any to go to the movies.

I went last year on his big day and will go next year too. Six is everybody's evil number. I have to get this anniversary over with as quickly as possible.

Maddie called again this morning to beg me to visit. Her thick voice is still on the machine. It's midnight where she is. She never mentions John.

She'll be asleep now. I don't have to call her back. If she's staying up all night she'll try again soon.

I never get over the excitement of taking my coffee out of the freezer every morning! Scooping it into the percolator, lighting the flame, anticipating euphoria.

The scissors caught my eye as I was waiting. Scissors are sexy when they're cutting something. For some reason they cheer me up. When I'm in a bad mood or if I just fancy something to do, I'm fond of snipping away with my sharp silver scissors. There's something exhilarating about destroying things. Old letters can't be read before being ripped with the blade. Never look at a photograph before cutting it up.

9

The pictures in the box under the bed are all of John. His short life is well documented. Our father fancied himself as a photographer and when Maddie inherited grandfather's money, she bought F a dead expensive Nikon and a newfangled cine-camera.

With my eyes shut, I pick six pictures out of the box. Looking forward to the cheery sound of the snips, cutting up my guilt — like the big scissors in Spellbound *when Greg Peck dreams about his dead brother. As I slash John's cheek or amputate his leg, I can see myself in the mirror. 'You two look dead alike,' our friend Lolita used to say, 'except you're beautiful and he's strange.'*

This ritual can't go on for ever. There aren't that many photographs left. When they run out, my habit will die an unnatural death. Either that, or I'll get bored with snipping and decide to paste the remaining pictures into a red leather album.

In the mirror, my face is pale and clean and tired. Even though I'm refusing to look at John, I can see him too. Since nothing is allowed to contradict my memory he will always be Montgomery Clift in A Place in the Sun: *flawed and mesmerizing and doomed. Every time I watch that movie, John's disfigured soul shows in Monty's immortal face.*

If Elizabeth Taylor hadn't outlived her beauty, I'd still be identifying with her. Death is a movie fan's best friend. Ava and Vivien and Marilyn and Marlene and Hepburn and Hayworth and Harlow can't pop up on soap Oprah. *They managed to die young, thin or mysterious. You only see them when the lights go out.*

It always surprises me to hear about the death of a goddess on the news. Some vintage Hollywood star you thought was already in Heaven. Icons can't die! Death confirms their immortality because they're impossible to replace. They are always there for you when you want them and when you need them.

Once I was soothed, I sifted the waste bits of picture into the middle of the bin, concealing John's tactile vulnerability under used razors, blood-stained tissues and champagne bottles. It's amazing that something feeble like paper can ruin something perfect like scissors. In no time at all, they need sharpening again. Perfection is dead glamorous.

I never worry about being peculiar. Everybody's odd. The most common neurotic fantasy is pretending to be psychotic.

Blondes

'It takes a lot of time to be a genius you have to sit around so much doing nothing really doing nothing.'

Gertrude Stein

My autobiography of glamour begins the day Grandfather Money died.

Like John, Grandfather died suddenly. John's remains were discovered immediately. Grandfather Money's corpse wasn't found until the following afternoon.

We all lived in the same building, but he didn't like anyone going up to his flat on the top floor without an appointment. Every Saturday afternoon at three, my mother and her five blonde sisters gathered in his bedroom to drink tea and get on his nerves.

Mother, whose name is Maddie, was the only one who dared to bring her children. Even though we lived underneath him, we always arrived last because we had been delayed shopping.

That afternoon when we got out of the taxi – Maddie in her white Kim Novak coat, me in my Emma Peel catgirl outfit, John sulking – there was a fire engine, an ambulance and a police car in front of our building. Seven policemen blockaded the entrance. I couldn't smell burning. The paramedics looked bored.

Maddie screamed, 'Something terrible has happened!' She was always saying that, the mum who cried wolf.

A dark-haired detective in the ritual cheap blue suit said, 'Stand back – it's murder.'

Maddie fainted. Her coat slithered up her chicken legs as they dumped her on the stretcher. Opening one eye, she proved her identity by flashing her chequebook in the policeman's face. The crimplene suit took us to the sisters who were drinking Grandfather's whisky and crying in his kitchen.

'He was a clever man,' Vagina wailed. Sister Vagina's name is really Ruby, but she's called Vagina because of a messy gynaecological operation and a rumour (started by her husband) that she's frigid.

'Oh yes,' Maddie explained, 'your grandfather didn't trust dry cleaners. When his suit was dirty he always ordered a new one.' Maddie could hardly contain herself. It was a well-known fact that she was going to inherit all her father's money.

'A fascinating man,' sister Dolly agreed, puckering up her cartoon face.

'Forty-two years in his bed,' sister Dottie, the image of Diana Dors in a bad mood, said sourly.

'What did he need the suits for?' I asked.

'He went out at night,' Maddie said. 'Sometimes.'

'Where to?' They looked offended. None of them would admit that Grandfather went up to women in his pub and said, 'I'd like to get to know you in the biblical sense.'

'Mass,' Vagina said. Some laugh.

Sister Jenny's shoulders were shaking with mirth or hysteria. Sister Ivy, a dead ringer for Mae West with a mastectomy, eyed her with disgust. 'Give her a pill,' she said to Vagina.

While the sisters continued their demented chatterbugging, John and I went into the front room and switched on the television. Irene the Slut, the gorgeous seventh sister who escaped to New York, was sitting silently on top of it. She has the atmosphere of Russian vodka about her skin. Her ethereal eyes voice an eternal Fuck Off to her silly sisters. But even Irene was trapped by their trash puritan philosophies. By devoting her life to rebelling against them, her principal motivation remained reactionary. Instead of doing exactly what she liked – as they always accused her – she made a point of doing what they wouldn't like, then telephoning long distance to report the worst. If the garbage truck hadn't reversed through her windscreen and killed her while she was sitting in a jam between Fifth and Madison, Irene would have inherited Grandfather's money.

Grandfather was a slum landlord with the decency or bad taste to live in one of his own tenements, a charming East End building with a view of the gasworks. Maddie inherited a thousand of them. Insanely jealous of Irene, she sold the flats and invested the money in Grace Kelly handbags and holidays in the sun. After John died, she worked up the courage to emigrate to America, determined to wipe the floor with her dead sister in the glamour war.

When he jumped off the roof of Grandfather Money's building, Vagina said, 'I always knew that boy would come to a bad end.' We always called it Grandfather's building, even though by then Maddie had owned it for years. It's the only one she has left now.

The story was in all the papers. They used the picture of him looking like Montgomery Clift on the front page. His face came on the news the following night too, beautiful and hurt. Maddie couldn't understand it. 'Why did he have to do it here?' she kept asking. 'Of all the places to give me a showing up. Why? Tell me. Why here?'

'Of all the roofs in all the towns,' I said.

17

'Why did he have to spoil everything?'

'Suicide's dead glamorous,' I said.

'You're terrible.' She couldn't look at me. Her voice was sickening with guilt. 'You need your head examined.'

'Being brave makes life worth losing.'

'I haven't a clue what you're talking about.' She covered her powdered face with a white linen handkerchief.

'God for all anyone knows could be Cary Grant.'

'Today of all days you could make the effort not to talk double-dutch.' Maddie didn't look interested in my theory so I didn't bother explaining. Only a culture of decadent puritans can be certain that dying is definitely bad. John could be in Heaven right now having the time of his life.

'With your brains,' she said, 'you could have been a doctor and put a stop to all this nonsense.'

To kill time later, while she was deciding what to wear to the burning, I watched a video of *A Place in the Sun* – the movie that was on the smelly the day Grandfather Money's dead body was found. John had been sitting on the floor with me when the film started.

He got bored when Monty goes to the movies and meets Shelley Winters. From her first frame awful Alice Tripp has victim written all over her. When she's drowned on her honey-moon, it's a relief. And Shelley, who couldn't help getting fatter and fatter, perfected the victim role by rehearsing so hard in real life. You can just see her sitting on her sofa stuffing her face with cream puffs, remembering her parts from the alcoholic actress in *The Big Knife*, to the jealous mother in *Lolita*. She's perfect as the woman nobody wants to kiss twice.

Montgomery Clift was made for sacrifice. His pain is seductive. He doesn't know yet that he's going to crash his car

18

one night in the future when he leaves Elizabeth Taylor's house to drive alone down the mountain. He doesn't know how much he'll miss his beauty once it's spoiled.

But even though as George Eastman he's untarnished and adored, he's dying already. We're all dying from the minute we're born, but you can see his soul disintegrating. It's impossible to stop watching him. The only obligation an actor has is to be compelling. He makes you want to sob out loud. A man like that in real life would make you close your eyes or vomit.

John left the room, quietly passing through the hall and out the front door. He was always up on that roof watching the traffic while I, the wee vertigo victim, sat downstairs, safe. We had planned our roles already.

The film was almost finished when our father, a weak-chinned version of Paul Newman, returned from the pub to find his wife an heiress.

John and I called him Fuckwit behind his back. Maddie used to tell us to stop it and laugh. She married Fuckwit to 'walk all over him'. Now it annoyed her that other people could as well. But the sisters – who all hate their husbands – are too puritanical to divorce. Maddie sent Fuckwit to explain the loss of Grandfather to me and John because she wanted him out of her sight.

Fuckwit had been the last person to see Grandfather Money alive, on Friday night when he delivered his whisky. Grandfather was in bed complaining of a feeling of doom and a pain in his heart. I've never forgiven him for not walking into the sea when his wife died, in a perverted gesture of fidelity like James Mason in *A Star is Born*. At the last minute, the cameras would have stopped rolling – if he'd been prepared to make the gesture. Instead Grandfather went on living, clutching that cluttered heart. Now Fuckwit was overcome with sentimental guilt for not listening to the story he'd heard a million times.

John was called down from the roof. Some of the cousins had even infiltrated Grandfather's flat and were in the kitchen scoffing Fry's Cream on toast – a Money snack I didn't inherit a craving for. The ming was wafting into the front room. I stood up and shut the big door without taking my eyes off the screen.

'Grandfather Money has gone to Heaven,' Fuckwit said when John reappeared, carefully closing the door behind himself.

'You murdered my grandfather,' I said cheerfully. Never spontaneous with a reply, he fiddled with the top button on his Dirk Bogarde raincoat.

'Don't be upset,' he said mechanically. Upset? I was puzzled. Where *exactly* was Grandfather? In a coffin already? He was a card but I wasn't going to miss him. His bed stank and he'd hardly opened his mouth except to moan. Maddie had already come in and whispered to me, 'We're going to Paris!' It was a well-known fact that when she got her mitts on his money she was going to Paris to buy exactly what she wanted from the shops.

'I'm trying to watch this,' I said. Elizabeth Taylor, luminous and dramatic, has smuggled a newspaper into school. She's reading about Monty's death sentence. Tonight, I plan to climb the ladder to John's bunk, lips stained with raspberry ice-pole, and practise kissing him. And when I get my new room – 'the minute Grandfather goes, you'll get your own room,' Maddie had been promising for ages – it's definitely having a mirrored wall like the one in Angela/Elizabeth's room at the lake. We were going to live in a big white house in the West End too, but she was scared the sisters would go off her so we moved upstairs to Grandfather's roomy flat instead. Our old place downstairs was rented to 'a stranger' to save the sisters fighting over it.

Fuckwit turned the sound down on the smellyvision.

'Mummy!' I screamed. Maddie came running in and turned the sound back up for me. 'The wee one's happy as Larry,' she said, 'so long as she has her movie.' Larry, her brother, had drowned at sea. He wasn't named after Olivier, which is just as well, because Lord Larry's publicized turd-burgling activities with Danny Kaye – of all people – spoiled the name for future generations of star-worshippers. 'Don't sit so close to the screen,' Maddie warned, lifting me back. Fat Spam isn't the full banana from sitting too close to the smelly. Vagina blames her daughter's cheap, available and disgusting ways on that early experience with our telly.

Vagina came to poke her red nose in. 'Are you sure that tiara's not squeezing her wee brain?' she asked. I was in the habit of wearing my fake diamond tiara to watch movies. Putting it on helped me concentrate, like the lights going down in the cinema. Maddie was forced to carry it around in her bag, just in case. For years it was my ambition to have a real tiara. Maddie had promised to get me one, 'If you're really good and we can find a shop with decent ones.' By the time I saw diamond and emerald platinum tiaras on display in a window in Bond Street, I'd gone off the idea. My idea of glamour had outgrown the chi-chi princess look.

'There's nothing small about my brain,' I said. John sniggered. Maddie slapped the side of his head. Fuckwit looked at her.

She said, 'He makes me nervous.'

'The wee one accused me of murder,' Fuckwit whispered as Monty Clift was led to the electric chair, knowing exactly what time he's going to fry. Most of us have to guess. You don't see him being executed. You feel it when The End appears across his face.

'Tell her I didn't do it,' Fuckwit said. 'Maddie, tell her.'

Good looking but pointless, Fuckwit's a man who always manages to find grief in good fortune. Instead of fantasizing about the vulgar rich person's Rolls Royce he'd been promised, he was sitting there working up his guilt.

'Your daddy didn't do it,' Vagina said. 'It was a bad man.' Vagina made a point of sticking up for Fuckwit because her husband had named his budgie after Maddie. On New Year's Eve, Vagina always managed to talk Fuckwit into doing an Esther and Abi Ofarim duet which disgusted everybody: 'You're the lady, You're the lady, That I love, You're the lady, The lady oooo . . .'

A burglar had given Grandfather a fright. His heart stopped. 'A heart attack,' the doctor called it, but it wasn't a heart that attacked him. It was a man with a stocking over his head. Nowadays, burglars keep regular hours. They break in during the day while you're out shopping. The stocking craze is out of fashion. But in those days, burglars in Glasgow worked the night shift.

Grandfather had died as he had lived: in his bed. In all the photographs we have of him he's an old man sitting up in bed with a glass in his hand. He took to his bed when he was forty and his wife, Maria, an anorexic girl with straight shoulders, died of consumption. After Maria's death he had sex with my grandmother but didn't marry her. Grandmother Dolly wasn't glamorous, she was 'too good', which means she was treated like a doormat. She was fat and working class and died just before I was born. Maddie blamed this foetal experience for my dark hair in a family of blondes. Giving me a sentimental smile, she patted my hair, saying to Vagina, 'Thank God she has blue eyes at least.'

'Poor wee thing,' Vagina said. 'What movie are you watching, pet?'

'I don't know the name of it,' I said perversely. I wasn't going to discuss it with her. She was fuming because Maddie was taking me on the Parisian spending spree.

'All that Hollywood stuff's made up,' she said scornfully.

That makes it better! These days, if Vagina read newspapers she'd be agreeing with critics who complain that Quentin Tarantino is more influenced by old movies than his old life. As if a broken heart or a mental breakdown automatically makes better material than an obsession with *Kiss Me, Deadly!*

While the crumblies were chatterbugging, I sneaked into Grandfather Money's big bedroom. The midnight-blue curtains were drawn. The lump under the bedclothes wasn't moving.

Blue-tinted Maria was sitting serene on his bedside table, her translucence gleaming in the dark. Even though her transparent body had never been deformed by childbirth, the sisters were always accusing me of looking like her. Maria's hair was the colour of muck as well. Muck makes you think of coffins, but bleach makes you think of ravished angels and there's nothing more painful than tarnished purity. The sisters were always going on about my hair.

'If it gets any darker,' Vagina said, 'it will be impossible to dye blonde.'

'It'll go that coarse yellow colour,' Dolly said. Take a look in the mirror, clown-face.

'People will think she's not your child,' Ivy was always saying.

'What sort of life is she going to have?' Dottie asked. Have they never heard of Hedy Lamarr, Ava Gardner, Vivien Leigh?

John tiptoed into the room and stood beside me, the hairs on his arms grazing mine.

'Did you look?'

'Yes,' I lied, pulling down my PVC sleeve.

23

'Prove it.'

'Shut up.' He knew I couldn't resist a dare. Quickly, I grabbed the cover off Old Money's face. Terror was written all over his gaping eyes and mouth. He didn't have his teeth in.

'Oh no,' I said. 'Where are his falsies?'

'I've got them,' John said, pulling them out of his pocket. 'They were on the table.'

'Dead morbid,' I said, and then, 'Oh-o.' My legs disappeared. The floor cracked my head open. When I came round Maddie was kneeling beside me shrieking, 'My God, she'll be scarred for life!'

She bought me a diamond ring to make up for the trauma.

At Grandfather Money's funeral John and I stood close together trying not to giggle out loud.

'It's a disgrace,' the sisters said, fat backs curved against the cold. They thought Maddie had a nerve bringing us to witness the mahogany coffin being lowered into its muddy pit. Their yellow-blonde hair was concealed beneath enormous umbrellas as they stood in the drizzle feeling bitter. They were all the same as each other, big and clumsy and envious.

Even then Maddie was anxious to escape to her place in the sun but being cowardly she had to spend years first weighing up the disadvantages, until John gave her the final shove. She stood grasping a handkerchief, wearing sugar-pink lipstick and her first BlackGlama, aware that everyone wanted to stare at her.

I couldn't distract my attention from the hole even though I wasn't looking at it. When I took a quick peek, it seemed absurdly large. He was really going to be left down there! Grandfather wasn't a nice man but I liked him. You can afford to be indulgent about people you're not forced to live with. He was really old when he died. Experiencing John's death left an echo in my soul. Only on days when I wake up feeling tragic.

Grandfather's grave had been lined up for him for ages, a family crypt 'full of old friends', as Maddie put it – an odd way to describe your rellies.

She had John burned because the sisters said, 'He's unholy.' Vagina, who always wanted the last word, added, 'A suicide is never welcome in Heaven.'

How would she know?! I bet she's never had a wee chat with God in her life.

Grandfather Money's do was held at his hotel.

The sisters were ashamed of The Golden Fountain. Its rooms weren't used for sleeping in. There's no water in the fountain these days. They begged Maddie to get rid of the place as soon as possible, but had the do there because of its proximity to both the city centre and cemetery. Grandfather had too many admirers for the scotch and smoked-salmon sandwiches to be served in his flat. And because the use of the ballroom wouldn't cost them a penny. Suddenly the sisters had started boasting about their poverty, trying to embarrass Maddie into sharing her windfall. She had agonized about 'splitting something six ways', but decided against.

'Your Grandfather Money wanted it this way,' she told me smugly.

People I'd never seen before in my life mingled with neighbours of ours dressed to the unrecognizable nines. The paraphernalia of celebration heightened the gathering, making an explosion inevitable amidst the purple flowers and painted faces.

Mr Uri, the manager – whose name was obviously extended to Urine – assembled the sisters in a line of grief. *Strangers in the Night* played discreetly as old women in mothy fur stoles filed past them, tearful. One said to Dolly, 'I was almost your mother.'

Dolly died shortly afterwards. She was spliced by a sash window, suffering a heart attack as she made the glass sparkly. The sisters always said, 'It was the shock of being singled out like that that killed her. That old bat definitely wasn't in with a chance with our father.'

Sister Dottie followed close on Dolly's heels, doing a Judy Garland by having her heart attack while sitting on the toilet. 'Constipation and fatty diets run in this family,' Maddie said when she heard the news.

Maddie, in her brand-new little black sleeveless Chanel cocktail mini-dress, was enjoying herself enormously. After the formalities, she moved between the blue velvet gilt chairs clutching a bottle of Laurent-Perrier, accepting kisses and compliments from the crumblies.

'It's dead glamorous, isn't it?' she asked me.

'If you say so.' I hadn't been to a funeral before.

'Where is that brother of yours?'

'I haven't a clue.' John was upstairs running along corridors. Too much alcohol turned Maddie into an emotional headcase. She always felt like slapping John when she was in a good mood.

Vagina, a rabid teetotaller – even though she looks like Barbie Windsor with a hangover – waited until Maddie was into her second bottle before saying aggressively, 'Money is the root of all evil.'

The whole room fell silent, waiting. Maddie's powdered face turned pink. All eyes were on her. She gave me the bottle, sobbing dramatically as she ran to the toilet. Accidentally on purpose I tipped the champagne over Vagina. She screamed like a wounded dog as it seeped into the man-made fibre of her outsize dress. Ivy, pleased with the confrontation, took the bottle off me saying, 'That child is out of control.'

Maddie was sitting staring at her face in the mirror. I picked up her pink lipstick, tossing it back in her bag. Who in their right mind wears pink?

'Looks open doors,' she said. She was terrified of losing her looks. Attention from men embarrassed her, but she had to keep her looks to taunt the sisters.

'Do you think I'm getting fat?' she asked, patting the roll of flesh circling her waist.

'You've always been fat.' I was still furious with her for holding me over Grandfather's decaying noggin in Mr Priceless the Undertaker's waiting room, where Old Money spent last night in his open casket, his blue hands clutching a cameo of Maria.

'You're her double,' Maddie had told me again. 'Now kiss your grandfather goodbye and don't take all day about it. He's the spitting image of God lying there.' I made a smacking noise with my lips, just managing to avoid the formaldehyde.

'Me, fat?' she arched her eyebrows. 'Rubbish! Black makes you look thin.'

'Being thin makes you look thin.'

'If you look fat in black there's no hope for you.' She stared in the mirror, a false grin spreading across her face. 'I don't know why I put up with you. Folk have told me I'm the double of that Grace Kelly.'

'I like the look of that orphanage.' This was one of our routines. The children's home in the park was a big white house with Scarlett O'Hara pillars lining the porch. Maddie wasn't sure if I was kidding or not. She wouldn't be able to stand the shame of a child who asked to be taken away from her.

27

'I wouldn't put anything past you,' she said. 'Do you want Mr Urine to make you a big knickerbocker glory?'

'Certainly not.' I couldn't bring myself to eat an ice cream with a name like that even if it does have a liqueur cherry on top.

'You're a wee bissum.'

'Don't call me that.'

'You're a rascal!' She lifted me by the armpits and swung me round to face the mirror. 'Where has that brother of yours got to?'

'He's hardly likely to be loitering in the Ladies room.'

'If you ask me,' she said, puffing Chanel amethyst on her nose, 'there's a bit of a woman about him.' Maddie's violent homophobia makes her accuse everyone she dislikes of being a biscuit. 'I'm thinner than all my sisters,' she said, checking her bum. Loose flab overcrowded the gap between her satin knickers and stocking tops. Exercise never occurred to her.

'Death has a funny effect on people,' she said.

'Ha, ha,' I said. Everyone is going to die. Tension builds as you wait for it to happen. Other obsessions kill time and camouflage that one big communal obsession.

'Don't screw your face up like that,' she said in a panicky voice. She was always warning me about gorgeous children who grow up to be pigs. There were a lot of them in her class at school. Imagining Maddie small was impossible. 'Even your Auntie Vagina,' she said in a voice full of omen, 'wasn't that bad looking when she was wee.' I glanced at my smooth face in the mirror. No wrinkles yet. Even paler than usual. We'd been up all night chattering again, shining our torches in the dark to break the monotony.

'You're like death warmed up,' Maddie said. 'Slap some of

this on.' She handed me her deep pink blush. I'd kill myself if I had rosy cheeks.

Ivy came to stick her oar in.

'Maddie,' she said, 'this is your father's funeral.'

'I know that,' Maddie sighed. She became distressed every time Ivy's moustache caught her eye. 'That thing's terrible,' she said.

'I can't do a thing about it.' Ivy's husband won't let her shave and depilatories bring her out in a rash that accentuates the 'tache as much as her violent orange lipstick. 'I know what you could do with her though,' Ivy glowered at me, 'get her a wee wig. That hair of hers is a disgrace. What will folk think? She looks nothing like a Money.'

'I know,' Maddie said, 'it's the colour of muck. But a wig's not the same as a bottle of peroxide.' She'd already had me in Fraser's trying on wigs.

'We'd better get back,' Ivy said.

Vagina had lined the sisters up for a photograph. They tried to drag me into it. Just before Mr Urine clicked the camera, I dodged out of the way.

It was time to go home. I found John and we jumped into the back seat of the hearse. Vagina and Maddie squeezed in beside us. 'You lucky wee dog,' Vagina said to me, 'going to Paris!'

'You look more like a dog than I do.'

'You're too smart,' she said.

'No one will ever say that about you.'

John didn't join in the chat. His silence disturbed them.

The espresso's buzzing through the percolator. It always takes me by surprise, even though I'm the one who prepared it. The phone's ringing again. It isn't her. Pour the coffee, take a sip.

29

Mmmmm. Smell. You can overdose on caffeine; what a great death.

Maybe I will visit Maddie. She's promised me 'a wee week in L.A., spending money, staying in a posh hotel, having a great time . . .' We may press on to her glass house in solar energy country, we may not. 'There are no shops in New Mexico,' she warned.

The face in the mirror frowns. 'You're the double of your mother when you do that,' the sisters used to say. Like Jack Kennedy's mum, they wore round-the-clock elastoplasts on their frown lines.

Dolly and Dottie had their heart attacks before having the chance to go abroad and moan. The remaining sisters, Vagina, Ivy and Jenny, have been Maddie's guests many times. They suspect she's living with a man in El Dorado. She met Jonathan the millionaire outside Pizza Hut, and goes red every time his name's mentioned. The closest the sisters have got to her house is Santa Fe, where she put them up in a hotel 'with lizards running the place'. Vagina nearly sat on one in the bath! It's hard to imagine a death more terrible than being squashed by Vagina's bum.

But it's definitely suspicious. Why did Maddie move there anyway? The rest of the retired beach babes go to Florida. When quizzed about this, Maddie said, 'I have no intention of having my handbag snatched.' She's in New Mexico 'being an artist', carrying the torch for her dead neighbours Tamara de Lempicka and Georgia O'Keeffe, supporting silver jewellery sales at the Indian reservation singlehandedly.

The sisters agree with Natural Born Bores, Mickey and Mallory, that New Mexico is brain-damagingly dull. They prefer to meet Maddie in San Francisco, 'where you can walk around', or L.A., where you can't.

30

'It's a disgrace' that I haven't been to see her yet, especially when she's offered (even though she's not rich any more) to pay the woman who used to bleach Marilyn's hair, and now does Madonna's, to tackle the impossible and blonde mine.

'I hate blondes,' John used to say at night after lights out, in the days when we shared a room before the inheritance. He pretended to be asleep when I climbed the ladder and practised kissing him.

What was the last thing he said to me? I haven't a clue. I can still hear him saying, 'I hate blondes.' And Robert De Niro's line from *Once Upon A Time in America*, 'No one will ever love you like I do.' He was good at impersonations.

The face in the mirror's impersonating me. It has John's eyes (same colour, different expression), Maddie's lips (same shape, different colour), the Money nose. The eyebrows I drew myself. The cheekbones were perfected by painful dentistry. A stolen face that like tomorrow belongs to me.

Most of the great faces invented themselves. Marlene painted a white spot on the tip of her nose, converting her square shape into an approximation of Garbo's more perfect oval. Dietrich, a middle-class *madchen*, pursued exoticism by spending all her money. Greta seduced her way out of the slums and stayed silent about it, keeping her cash under the bed, in suitcases, invested in real estate.

You can control your reflection. The angle, lighting and distance are organized mentally in advance of looking. It's the unexpected reflective surfaces that catch you out. The cashpoint machine, windscreen, computer lid, a blank TV that suddenly shows your face when the sun shines. These make the future unpredictable.

In the mirror today, even concentrating on selective areas – the good bits – I still look tired. I can't face Hollywood with this reflection. Before departure I need to organize an expensive excursion into the sensual sado-masochistic world of beauty treatments. A facial, a haircut, a fast, before travelling to the airport and getting on that plane.

Flying doesn't frighten me. I have always known that I will die alone in a car crash. Of course I could be making a mistake. There's a hideous possibility that I'll die in my sleep.

One thing's for sure. I can't hang around here all day waiting for the plot to thicken.

Today is definitely as good a day as any to go to the movies.

For a long time it's been my ambition to sit in a cinema alone. But even at the graveyard lunchtime screening, there are always one or two other souls sharing the stalls with me. As the day progresses, the cinemas of central London attract more voyeurs. The images on-screen respond to the way they are watched. During the day they send out spiritual reassurance reminiscent of taking communion with a small selection of strangers. At night these same pictures become more thrilling and threatening.

It would be rude to attend Mass with dirty hair, bending to receive the white wafer, leaving a perfume of grease. But the darkness of a movie theatre makes a speedy departure possible. This morning, as I left my building to rush to the cinema with my hair concealed under a Chanel-at-the-Races hat, I was wearing the ritualistic Firebrand lipstick essential for effective voyeuring. Even in a black-and-white movie, you can always be certain the heroine's lips are scarlet.

Today I'm going to see *The Last Seduction*, a colour noir, in the Curzon Mayfair. Brutally optimistic, I'm hopeful that maybe this time I'll be the only one to buy my ticket and sit in the seventh row. It's a popular film, but it's been on for a while. From the outside, the cinema looks as if bearded men go there to wank in the dark. Shepherd's Market, where Greta Garbo fantasized about dying in an automobile accident wearing a green hat, isn't really a neighbourhood for impulse viewers who wander in to kill time. The first show starts at lunchtime when office workers are eating their starchy snacks in small smokeless cafés. And on Maundy Thursday there's less people in London at a loose end. Today is the day for Easter preparations. Religious holidays are also the time most likely for Londonites to commit suicide. Living too long in a polluted city is supposed to make you desperate, but the screeches of barn owls terrorize me even more than travelling in taxis driven by garrulous maniacs.

Hurrying past the canal, the white stucco houses of Little Venice remind me more of a Hollywood set than they do of Big Venice. I wouldn't be surprised to see Kelly from *The Naked Kiss* coming out of one of them, her proud face stained with determined tears. Her millionaire boyfriend's a child molester. Kelly had to kill him even though the obscurity that accompanies poverty is a terrifying conclusion even to a fantasy.

Instead of Constance Towers, an actress I've only seen in Sam Fuller movies, I saw Sadie the Slink standing on the bridge staring at the stagnant water. A *femme fatale* who reeks of Weimar and cigarettes, she suits her hair in its Dietrich parting. As she leans forward, her fringe falls over her serious face. Death by Stolichnaya would suit her better than death by drowning.

'I feel uncomfortable around mirrors,' slinky Sadie told me last week in a toilet. She would be better in a movie than real life, but doesn't like being photographed. When I was young, I used to dance naked to her records with my best friend Lolita,

33

who fancied John. John hated his name but couldn't be bothered changing it; Lolita was really Linda. Now she's a go-go dancer and still calls herself Lo and isn't my best friend any more. Sometimes we meet by chance in cinema foyers and recognize the movie junkie in each other. She boasts with embarrassment and pride about her next Soho striptease.

'I'll get you on the guest list,' she promises, 'if you want to come see me dance.'

Lolita and those other faces from the past search my expression for tragedy. Know any suicide jokes? Did you hear the one about the brother who jumped off the building? Oops, forgotten the punchline.

The sisters said, 'It's a disgrace. He's the first member of the Money family to do the devil's work.' Now that I'm older and more idealistic, I envy John even more than I did the day he did it. Having courage like that is dead glamorous. There's no charm in stiffupperlipping along waiting for the worst. He was brave enough to do the one thing he'd always longed to. You don't have to want to kill your self to identify with that ambition.

When we were young John suggested a suicide pact. Even though the idea of dying together was romantic, self-destruction attracts me purely as a voyeur. John was a suicide junkie for years before he cured himself.

The Moneys are a family of junkies.

Everyone's obsessed with something. Maddie and her sisters are all Nazis. They survived World War Two living a stone's throw from the gasworks, a favourite target of Goering's gorillas. The sisters believe themselves to be patriotic, but each of them is suffused with the fascist traits of fanaticism and fetishism. There's a ritual and a rule for everything.

They dislike their children but pride themselves on being

perfect mothers. They spend their days pursuing sexy glamour, but refuse to shag their husbands. They consider driving to be 'unfeminine'. Maddie was forced to pass her test when she emigrated, but even in the land of convertibles and car crashes she always has a man drive for her when the opportunity arises. The sisters were over the moon that Irene the Slut had come to a bad end in the red Ford Mustang that Grandfather had bought her. There was a rumour that nymphomaniac Irene, who looked like Sharon Tate and led a Valley of the Dolls existence – dancing all night, getting up at noon – may even have slept with a Chinaman . . . *on a regular basis.*

'Can you think of anything worse?' Maddie obsessively asked Vagina. Vagina doubled her chin into her neck and shook her head, livid with shock even though they'd discussed the subject a million times.

The hereditary addictive personality doesn't worry me. For years I invented an immaculate escape from the gene pool, pretending they were nothing to do with me. Now I'm relaxed with my own addictions. One day it's speedy organic Buzz bars, another it's champagne-tequila. These shop-bought thrills enable me to avoid the bourgeois world of illegal drug consumption. Most thrills have a shelf life but the movies are always there for me.

There's a torn cinema ticket in my pocket for a midnight movie I saw with John in New York. Impossible to discard or idolize, I'm forced to leave it in there. Forgetting has to be easy. If it takes too much effort you may as well remember.

A close-up of Princess Diana's face decorates the station kiosk, but I don't need a tabloid – I heard the latest gossip on TV, and I don't want the photograph. Is she boring, brainless, bland? I hope so.

The woman's a walking death metaphor! Diana and her supermodel sisters aren't the new Hollywood goddesses. Those girls are the living dead, not the immortal dead. Mortality lurks too close to the surface of their imperfect skin. It's their emptiness that's attractive. Necrophilia is appealing. They know they're not good enough to be immortalized, and that insecurity of the soul makes it possible for them to be transient icons. Frantically, they grab at a movie role – then open their mouths and make fools of themselves.

While Naomi Campbell and Kate Moss are dancing in New York nightclubs, it's possible to imagine Saint Diana lying awake underneath her satin sheets, thinking about the fate of Louise Brooks or Veronica Lake. Louise sold perfume in Bergdorf Goodman after her stint as the Lost Girl; but she ended up alone and alcoholic and immortal because the celluloid proof had already been preserved. Veronica Lake's last job was mixing cocktails in a hotel bar, but she's remembered driving her car through the rain in *The Blue Dahlia*.

Diana's battered innocence is her last ally. The only hope for her is to become a heroin addict. Heroin is good glam fun for those who have the time and money and motive to indulge. And suicide would make her look like a copycat. The other members of the twentieth-century trinity, sex-goddess Marilyn Monroe and wounded mother Sylvia Plath, have already committed that immortal sin.

Diana has made death her best friend. Unlike the more beautiful Marilyn, or the clever Sylvia, her instinct has allowed her to exploit death culture without dying. Death is one thing that definitely interests everybody. The seductive associations of self-destructive behaviour are older than the addiction to peroxided hair.

Enjoying the living deaths of the famous is another way of

avoiding your own death. Watching the rich cry is more satisfying than seeing smug smiles. 'Everybody,' sings Liza Minnelli in *Cabaret*, 'loves a winner.' Really everybody loves a loser, so long as it isn't me.

I bought my ticket and descended to the platform, standing with one eye on the tunnel, one on a discarded *Sun*. Today's front page photograph reveals Diana's rough brown skintone. She's playing the maternal role too well. The virgin glow is gone. She's a mumsie blonde with a sagging smile. The sun-damaged skin makes my heart beat faster – stressing about all those winters and summers in the sun with Maddie, spending Grandfather Money's disappearing fortune.

Sun damage takes twenty years to appear and if the movies have taught me anything it's that you can only be adored if your complexion can stand the scrutiny of a key light. Your albino look has to travel with you, protected by hats in the summer and a knitted IRA mask in the winter, enabling you – like Marlene Dietrich – to show yourself off in the strategic lighting of your living room. It's hard work being gorgeous!

Forget all that rot about looks not being as important as the soul. That's exactly why they do matter: your soul shows in your face. Beauty and brains are just as likely a combination as ugliness and stupidity. Though other people's idea of beauty is usually disappointing. One man's *femme fatale* is another man's wan fatal. Glamour is more reliable. Harder to explain. Impossible to resist.

Diana's glamour was created by her fame. You would have looked once at her in the kindergarten, not twice. Now you would stare; or refuse to stare. Sucked in by Dianalust, or denouncing it to deny your need. First fascinated by her innocence, now her decay.

'She looks awful,' her blonde rivals say, ravenously scanning tabloids seeking out the shot-by-shot drama of disintegration. Up all night crying again, the loss of beauty is another reminder of death – your own death. If you were never beautiful, does that make it harder or easier to be alone in the dark? Whether you sleep nude or in pale satin pyjamas, lying down is always a rehearsal for death. Sleeping alone is terrifying because there's no audience. God, the invisible witness, never claps.

Diana worked as a char – in all the best houses – to make ends meet before her marriage. She scrubbed her sister's kitchen floor, then got to wear the Cinderellagown. But now she's on the wrong boat, she's going to disappoint me. Her addictions will never include morphine – even though it's supposed to be an excellent slimming aid. It didn't work for Bad Bob, my drug-dealing cousin, whose red leather jeans were always Extra Large.

Gym junkie Diana will never be a penniless size sixteen. But when she sees her face unexpectedly in the mirror she will be tempted to trace her hand over and over with a black pen on a piece of white paper. That bare hand, the one she refused to coat in a royal glove (so that the lepers could be seduced), reappearing on the page – an outline reminiscent of kinder-garten. The detail of her fingers reminds her that the bump made by the vulgar sapphire and diamond engagement ring has gone.

Quentin Tarantino has to give her a job! She can be the bloody beatific babe in his next movie. And between takes, while they're both waiting for something to happen, you can just see them comparing notes. From childminder to anyprin-cess; from video-store clerk to popular prophet. Oh yes, they could be married. His animated Neanderthal face would comple-ment her neurotic passive face. They'd have such a lot to fan-tasize about. But what if he doesn't propose? Worse, what if his racy noir camera doesn't adore her? There's already a suggestion of clumsiness in those big shoulders of hers.

However the plot twists, it's only a matter of time before Diana is photographed, hands covering her face, like Marilyn the day she announced her divorce from Joe DiMaggio. Why did Joe stop sending flowers? When Marilyn died – in the nude – he promised to send eternal red roses to her Westwood grave. Now he's cancelled the order.

There's never a good enough reason to stop loving a memory. It's painful to imagine him examining the florist's bill, a tear of regret staining his ugly Italian face. If I decide to see Maddie, I could visit Marilyn's grave. I can't take red roses. I'd have to pick yellow or white. I couldn't bear the compromise of pink.

One of the reasons I dread going: Maddie would want me to share a room with her. She's terrified of sleeping in a hotel room alone. 'Anyone can use a pass key and just let themself in and murder you in the middle of the night,' she told me on the inheritance tour. She used to stick a chair under the door handle before climbing into the bed next to mine.

'Glamour,' she whispered in the dark, 'is an exciting quality that arouses envy. Night, night, Angel.'

In the morning, while I was waiting for her to put her face on, I sat on the floor in Grand Hotel rooms in Paris and Vienna and Venice watching dubbed movies. The faces of actors were already important to me. This became a compulsion to study everybody's face, seeking those memorable images that provide insurance against death.

'It's not real,' Maddie told me, clutching a mascara wand. 'There's someone standing behind those people with a camera.'

I have always known that it is real. Hollywood, like Heaven and Hell, is a place of the imagination. Louise Brooks and Merle

Oberon and Liz Taylor can all be living on Sunset at the same time. Time is just another set, to be visited later. Soon?

As the train pulled into Warwick Avenue station, I was buying a Fruit and Nut from the machine: a good omen.

The glare in the compartment encouraged me to check my watch, afraid I'd miss the start of the movie. Rudolph Valentino was sitting opposite, his black hair glistening like liquorice under the brutal light.

Artificial lighting can expose or blank out the mistakes in faces. Shadows provide a dusky hush, murking mystery into make-up and skin tone. Daylight disturbs your calculations, switching from brash to shade, suiting itself.

Heart beating faster, I checked my watch again. I saw *The Last Seduction* already on the night flight back from New York. I've never understood that notion of only watching a movie once. I've been to Mass a million times but still enjoy the sensual rituals. Still, I hate to miss the opening credits.

The Rudolph Valentino look-alike was staring at the bruises on my left leg visible through my flesh-coloured nylons. 'Oh yes, the husband,' I confided, 'beats me.' I stumbled into an abandoned choc-ice tray in the aisle of the Warner West End but that sounds like a lie. Impossible anyway to explain in a put-down. He looked away, an agitated Latin impotent who can't think up a reply in time for my stop.

The Fruit and Nut was still sitting melting on the seat when I got off. He can have it for his lunch.

A fifties blonde with a sad smile reluctantly sold me my ticket. One of those women who became blonde with Marilyn but didn't outgrow it, she has taken offence at my hat. Blondes can't wear hats. After a false start, Diana more or less snubbed the hat. Marilyn wouldn't have been seen dead in one. And the other blonde, Sylvia Plath, had her bee-hat. She was cheated out of glamour by her brain, conned into thinking she had to chose one or the other: sex appeal or intellectual credibility. After her peroxide summer, Sylvia wasn't really blonde any more – but her place in the necrophiliac imagination makes her the third member of the unholy trinity.

I bought a hot white cup of effective black coffee that I was allowed to take into the auditorium.

Sitting in the middle of the seventh row, I'm defying John who always warned me to 'watch my back'. The air's clear and pure, the seat comfortable. Other people are nearby but I can't see them yet. Watching a movie is like having a wee chat with God: best done alone. But you can be too reverential. Maybe one of these days I'll be able to go to a cinema in a crowd and have popcorn fights.

The ads. Absolut Vodka, yum, yum. A colourless odourless shot with an invisible twist of corrupting lime. In real life I prefer Stolichnaya.

Bacardi and Pepsi. Excellent. Unlike other children of alcoholics, I enjoy a rollick. Abstinence is its own punishment. Moral highbrow acts are tiring. Because of my illness nowadays I have to stick to champagne – known as tonic in our family. 'Is the tonic in the fridge or the freezer?' we ask each other, searching for the missing bottle.

There was a lot of tonic at Grandfather's funeral but none at John's quieter do. 'There's nothing to celebrate,' Vagina informed Maddie when she was considering ordering a crate to soften the blow, 'that boy is definitely damned.'

*   *   *

41

Some movies pass in a daze, provoking memories. Even a rotten movie can act as a catalyst to the imagination, distracting your attention from the screen. When the jolly intro music starts, it's like the Priest walking in. You sit up straighter, stomach muscles tense. I have to tell a man behind me to Shut Up. He's breathing too loud for fun.

Watching a movie is a seductive experience, but not every movie! It's like that question: 'Do you like children?' What, all of them? Cinema audiences have doubled in the last decade. Like sexual love, the attraction to particular movies is partly mysterious and beyond analysis. You can fall in love with an actor, a setting, a theme tune. You can never be sure which detail, trivial or profound, makes it indelible. It's as impossible to separate as death and glamour.

Linda Fiorentino, a *femme fatale* with Kate Moss thighs, is Bridget in *The Last Seduction* but also Rachel in *The Moderns*. Rachel is beautiful but she has no money. She marries a poor man and a rich man and secretly loves the poor man. Scott Fitzgerald could have warned her that poor girls can't marry poor boys, but she had to learn the lesson in twenties Paris herself.

The Last Seduction gets off to a hot start. Bridget (like Brigitte) is a high-heel junkie. She has a Double Indemnity parting to her dark hair and steals a carrier bag full of money in the first five minutes.

Rachel's vaguely bruised innocence has hardened into a fantasy of self will. Bridget the bitch avoids being beat-up or having her loot taken away from her. She controls all the men in the movie. In real life, threats and fate can't always be manipulated by smart-thinking and sexy smiles. A good movie tricks by appearing to be subtle while offering simplistic solutions. Believe what you want to believe. Darkness helps.

There's nothing about Bridget that makes you stop believing in Rachel. Directors instinctively understand this when they typecast. Bridget manages to be different from Rachel without destroying her. Looking at Bridget reminds me only of Rachel — not of Linda, the actress.

The best actors give everything. Keeping themselves empty, living down to the audience's expectations. In real life it's essential to avoid what's expected of you for as long as possible. Responsibility kills the soul.

Bit by bit, the parts you play influence your life and lead like every other route to death. Maddie spent a fortune finding herself when she should have concentrated on losing herself. She ran away but can't escape, terrified the sisters won't like her any more if she stops bleaching her hair and wearing black seamed stockings to the supermarket.

Bridget's seductive and destructive but not self-destructive. John was successfully self-destructive. Maddie failed in her continued attempts to be seductive. You can only be truly self-destructive once. Acting seductive becomes an embarrassing habit after the first twenty years.

Bridget commits a glam movie murder with courage but without conscience or consequence. Real-life murderers are cowardly. Bad Bob, a son of Ivy's she always said 'wouldn't harm a fly', did a murder. Not a fly — his best friend, who had stolen his drugs. A murder like that does nothing for the imagination. And in his cell, Bad Bob will be sitting on his bed too lazy to swat any flies that manage to buzz in through locked windows.

There's nothing apathetic about Bridget. She achieves her objectives with a smile, wearing tight black forties skirts and well-cut tops. She's skinny and sexy and brainy. At the end, she's driven off, unpunished, in her limousine by a chauffeur who only speaks when spoken to. Like cool Clarence in *True Romance*, Bridget should be dead. But reality is over-rated and often irrational anyway.

The rules of cinematic glamour have been drilled into me like a catechism, to be reinvented and applied to real life. The Rank starlets went to Charm School; I had film noir. And trash noir, cult noir, classic noir. From cool blonde to slut blonde, brunette babe to Fu Manchu, *Naked Kiss* to *Reservoir Dogs*, movies taught me about sudden wealth, sudden death, love at first staircase.

Pale-skinned beauties walk down marble staircases wearing fitted satin evening gowns. There's a bit of madness or sadness in their past, the future is either ecstatic or tragic. Compromise is repellent.

I wanted to live in a black-and-white world with champagne for breakfast and millions of men committing suicide over me. And the real world turned out to be the same as the movies. Life did work out the way the glamour age of Hollywood promised.

Maddie's inheritance confirmed the sudden wealth scenario. In real life millionaires keep their money, growing more; but Maddie — like an invented heroine — spent hers.

John's suicide validated the sudden death drama, though he'd been rehearsing for years — inspired by the performances of Marilyn and Sylvia and Sid. By livening up reality, art makes death possible.

I grew up and married Dangerous Donald, a blond I met in an elevator. We have the white-carpeted apartment, but not the black maid.

Movies steal from life and life imitates movies. Imagination is prophetic.

*   *   *

The audience abandon their seats and stumble into the artificially lit foyer, furtive, not wanting to be witnessed with nothing better to do than be at a movie early in the afternoon.

Escaping into the sunlight, I feel pale and hungry – as if something astonishing has just happened.

Great-aunt Carmen, a woman I've chatted to before who never recognizes me, catches up with me.

'Did you enjoy the movie, dear?' she asks, snapping her bag open and shut. Give someone a name and they try to live up to it.

'Oh yes.'

'It was a real pleasure but I felt sorry for the chap in the end.' The cowboy who pays for Bridget's sins. 'I shall worry about him tonight as I'm trying to sleep.' She indulges a smile. 'You see, I'm an insomniac.' She told me that last month at the popcorn counter of the Chinese rep before a 4 pm screening of *Reservoir Dogs*. 'Every night I have to wait until at least midnight before my sleep train comes.'

'You could watch the late movie.'

'I don't go out at night, dear,' she says, fiddling with her bag to show off its clasp, reminding me of Tippi Hedren in *Marnie*.

'There's usually one on TV.'

'Oh no,' she looks horrified, 'it's not the same on the television, dear.'

'An original Kelly?' I enquire, admiring the lizard handbag. For only two thousand dollars you too can have one. The long-handled design can be used as a shoulder bag or hung precariously on the wrist the way Maddie used to swing hers, convenient for accidentally-on-purpose bashing me in the ear.

'Oh no, Radio Rentals,' Great-aunt Carmen replies. 'Half of all the films ever produced are gone for ever,' she says. Adding,

'You must come to my house some time, dear.' She makes her exit, an elegant little woman wearing seamless bottle-green leather silk-lined gloves on a summer's day; dangling the hand-bag as if she covets something else to put inside it.

Back at my building, there's another long-distance message from Maddie.

I can see her sitting in the morning sun, impatiently punching her phone. When she gets through she'll demand, 'Where the Hell have you been?'

And I can give her the glad tidings. I'm visiting her at last.

Diana's on the news again, climbing into her car, hiding behind of all things a tabloid. Her skin, a living organism, is dying. Freeze the image and examine the cracks at the edges of her too-blue eyes, the droop to the left and right of those unkissed lips.

'She faces a future of lunching, shopping and holidays,' the newsreader says, as if she'd automatically be happier committed to charities or charring. Diana has to be either fulfilled or frivol-ous. Anyone without a career is frittering away their life. A career involves an alarm clock and a relationship with public transport. It's worthwhile because it pays.

Yet you can look as if you're doing nothing, and actually be practising being a saint or sage. Glamour, like God and your past, is lurking everywhere – even when it's denied. True devotion to an obsession takes a leap of faith, a lot of free time, and an easy income.

Committed obsessives in their extremity help create an atmosphere that alarm clock people can participate in when escapism is essential or desirable. Glamour hunger, the need for icons and absolutes, is rife because even its ambiguities are

clear-cut. Glamour is another word for seduction. Everybody
wants to seduce, be seduced, or gain power resisting.

Next time she called I picked up the phone.

'Where the Hell have you been? I thought you were dead!'

'Work,' I lied.

'At this time of day?'

'There was somebody off sick.'

'That's a funny job you've got. I've never heard of anything
like it. Have Fortnum's delivered your egg yet? I warned them
you won't eat it unless it's wrapped in blue foil. I have to tell
them that every year. What are you having for dinner on Easter
Sunday?'

When I could get a word in, I told her the good news.

'My God,' she said. We managed to discuss the details without falling out. We're going to meet in L.A. for no more than
seven days. I'm allowed my own room so long as we have a
suite and I promise faithfully to sleep with the connecting door
open. During the day we'll have time to 'do our own thing'
but we'll still see a lot of each other. After all, it's only seven
days. Everybody's lucky number.

'You don't have your fingers crossed behind your back?' she
asked nervously after I had promised twice. 'When are you
coming?'

'Soon,' I said.

Filling a silence, she said, 'You used to be a wee Hollywood
addict. Do you ever go to the movies these days?'

Spellbound

Time slows down and speeds up to suit itself. Watching a movie in the morning is different from the afternoon. Some of the best movies are on before noon these days, when I'm the only one watching. If Dangerous Donald was home, I wouldn't be able to sit through the whole show. We'd start talking, or go out for breakfast, or have a pillow fight.

Eleven o'clock. Second post will arrive any minute. I'm fast-forwarding through *Vertigo*, looking at Kim Novak's grey suit. There's a scene near the end where a mannequin walks in wearing a similar suit that isn't quite The Suit necessary to fuel James Stewart's obsession. I'm planning a suit of my own. Same style, richer colour. Or maybe I should go for an impossible identical copy?

Time is serene in San Francisco, insane in New York. Time is vertiginous, mixing itself up. Fantasy is the future – it can seem real or impossible in the present. Memory and lies are the past. It's a different time in L.A. than it is in London. Clocks move backwards and forwards when the season changes, and can be moved or stopped at any time too – when you want to fool yourself into thinking it isn't time to get up; or warn yourself it's time to have a good time.

Even when you can't see light or darkness outside, am time feels different from pm time. Even though my thick velvet curtains are closed, and the black-out blind's down, it still feels like morning.

Money from Maddie and a padded envelope from Fuckwit arrived in the afternoon post.

Promises are made to be kept, but I've been making excuses for months. *I'm sick. I can't afford the trip. I'll come after Christmas.*

Now I have the money. It's a New Year. I have to go?

The photograph she sent with my travel expenses proves that Maddie has kept her promise to avoid plastic surgery.

'I am no narcissist,' she is fond of saying. 'My good looks are natural.'

There she is, blonde and painfully tan, hunched against the wall of her glass house. Solar energy, it would be 'a shame to waste all that sunshine' because she has 'no intention of getting to know anyone else'. Jonathan the Millionaire is out of the picture. This means she can shrivel her skin till her heart's content; no man will ever see her naked. Living in terror of sexual perversion, but still making herself up like a tart.

Even though – as she keeps reminding me – she's poor these days, she's sent me enough for a first-class ticket, a leather suitcase and the clothes to put in it. When we did the inheritance tour, everything in our new leather suitcases had to be new. Not for her the elegance of faded grandeur, she felt embarrassed at the idea of wearing something twice while living in an hotel. 'I'd die if people thought we were poor,' she kept saying.

She can't resist enclosing motherly advice. *For God's sake, don't forget to have a manicure.* And, *I know you have queer taste, but try to buy at least one smart outfit – we might bump into the President!*

Ronald Reagan used to stay at The Ambassador Hotel, where she's booking us a suite. *Kings Row* is one of Maddie's favourite movies. She loves the bit where his legs are sawn off. *I can't get into Bill Clinton at all*, her letter continues, *he's far too fat to be a philanderer.*

Maddie is not divorced from Fuckwit, who still lives in the family flat in Glasgow where my bedroom is 'just the same' though I haven't seen it for seven years. The paint, the furniture, the carpet, are white like Heaven. The mirrored wall converts it into two rooms. The window overlooks the main road that's always thick with traffic. It used to be Grandfather Money's room. 'The wee one's dead morbid,' Maddie said, when I insisted on having that room. I chose it because it's the biggest.

I was the first person in my class to have a lock on my bedroom door. Me and John and Lolita used to bolt ourselves in there whether we were recording secrets on my cassette player or not.

I keep the giant key to my old room in a safe place. I see it when I open my jewel box to check that everything's still there. The ruby bracelet Maddie gave me after my illness, the piece of broken glass from the mirror in my old flat, the antique locket John sent me. Dangerous told me, 'Older brothers usually ignore their sisters.' John and I were close in age and often taken for twins. The colour has faded out of the bit of hair in the locket. It could belong to either of us. I can see the scissors snipping it off his head, a memory of a sight I didn't witness.

I wouldn't dream of listening to the tapes of us talking. They would make me cringe. Lolita's Scottish accent is still really strong, even though she's lived in London almost as long as me.

'If you hadn't gone to acting school, we would never have

split up,' she said when we met accidentally last week in the Everyman's basement toilet. I had stumbled downstairs, disorientated by the movie, and gashed my ankle on the bottom step.

'My God, you're bleeding,' she said, her wee face fraught with concern. She kneeled down to get a better look at the blood smeared above my black sock. She hadn't been my best friend for ages before I went to New York. John had never really liked her anyway. Now she's an extra from the past who insists on trying to make us the stars of her epic tragedy. You can't let a role in someone else's fantasy wear you out. She knew for a fact I'd be here today. I can't resist *Naked Kiss* in a cinema. Concentrating on it in the dark is different from watching a video. It isn't just the big bold screen that makes the difference. The temptation of the pause button when the phone rings is too much, and an interrupted movie is like a half-hearted kiss.

'I fell downstairs.'

'Is that the foot with the tubercular toe?'

'No,' I lied.

'Your dancing days are over.' She smiled, offering me a tissue. My famous year in bed with my tubercular toe caused severe muscle wastage. My legs will never be the same again, no matter how many high kicks I do before breakfast. The toe's scarred and clumsy now but no longer suppurating with pus. It's great having an excuse to carry a walking stick. 'But you're every bit as thin as you used to be.'

'You sound like my mum,' I said, half-heartedly dabbing the blood. I'm a middle-aged woman's idea of thin, not a hairdresser's.

'How is Maddie?'

'Still sunbathing.'

51

'She used to be furious with us for jumping on the bed, remember?' The three of us used to jump on the big bed in my room, ruining the springs. The loony husband in Fritz Lang's *Secret Beyond the Door* makes the mistake of obsessively visiting a replica of his dead wife's room. Asymmetrical candles disturb his sanity in the shameful shrine. The copy-cat set has to be destroyed for the sake of a happy ending with Joan Bennett, his wanky new wife, whose eyes bulge with pretend hysteria in every frame but the last.

If Fuckwit died, I would have to revisit my room and destroy my possessions. Everyone's been expecting him to die for years, trapped up there at the top of the building with his alcohol dependence and pointless future. But he never dies, he waits. When I was young I prayed every night for his death. The sound of them screeching at each other, competing with the television, got right on my nerves. But now I want him to go on existing. Because I know that parents stave off your death by connecting you to your birth. Their deaths are shocking whether you love them or not.

My room gives him an excuse to keep in touch with me. He doesn't like talking to machines. He sends messages in block caps on blue Basildon Bond at this time of year, in the no man's land between winter and spring. HOPEFULLY WE CAN RESOLVE OUR INDIFFERENCES. (Hysterical.) I KNOW YOU HATE ME. (Self-pity.) And, still to come, the obscene: HAPPY BIRTHDAY I LOVE YOU.

Dangerous chortles over these notes with me but even though he never says it out loud I know he wonders why I can't be kind and reply. It's hard enough staying in contact with Maddie and having to remember John without encouraging someone that I never loved. Pretending to love rellies is the same as pretending to hate them. It corrupts your soul. God's love is infinite. Mortal love isn't strong enough to dilute too many times.

When I was small I loved my mum and I can't get out of the habit of John. Everyone I know is called John, even Dangerous Donald has the initial J lurking on his chequebook, though he's always Dangerous when he says his name out loud. He pays for presents with his credit card. For bills, he writes cheques. I like watching him write, a slow frown of concentration on his amber brow. At first I thought of him as blond John, and the first John as black John. But now he's Dangerous Donald even in my imagination.

No one calls our father John. He's referred to as F nowadays, a face-saving ambiguity: F for Father or Fuckwit. Maddie keeps in touch with him, out of perversity, but doesn't stay in the flat when she goes to Glasgow on her spur of the moment showing-off sprees. She books a suite in Devonshire Gardens, 'the in hotel' according to both her and Alex my film-maker friend, who videos a lot of Scottish popstars.

F heard about the maternal reunion from Aunt Vagina, who lives downstairs. She 'refuses to go near him, you should see what he looks like these days', but occasionally bumps into him in the close as he staggers, stinking, into the building. 'Maria is going to visit Madeleine,' she told him. The sisters call me Maria because of my pious childhood and my famous resemblance to Grandfather's first wife.

'I find that hard to believe,' F stammered. In a gesture of rivalry, he has sent me a film of my past in the brown padded envelope. Taken on super-8, it was badly edited before its conversion into video in a crude attempt to cut John's scenes. THEY MAY CAUSE YOU PAIN. His character nonetheless emerges in the moments when he's standing too close to me to be effaced. In a thirty-minute film, his unforgettable face is visible at least seven times. There he is dressed as a TV set at Halloween, sobbing beneath the cardboard box while I dance aggressively beside him, only pausing to puff my joke-shop cigarette. Here he is again, screaming blue murder as Grandfather Money's train pulls out of the seaside station while I smile, wave, and take consecutive licks of the two 99s I'm grasping expertly in one hand. Then we're travelling down a chute – me full of manic glee; him sombre, worrying we might go flying off the edge at the bottom and crack our heads on the concrete like our fatneck cousin did the week before. The camera follows me as I race back up the stairs, desperate to slide down again. I look like I'm on drugs.

At my third birthday party he looks happy in a striped convict t-shirt. I have an early-period Liz Taylor hair-do, worn with Ava Gardner's almond eyes. We're sticking our fingers into the enormous pastel cake. Licking the icing, then stealing more as my pet pooch observes silently. John whispers something to me and smiles. Our secret. There's something insane about my shoulders.

Maddie's starring moment comes in profile as she applies her make-up, gazing at the mirror with ferocious concentration, oblivious that her panic-stricken vanity is being immortalized by a man she doesn't love. Her nose is enormous. Her half-naked cheekbones never looked so much like Old Money's. In fact, beneath her beauty, the masculinity in her bone structure is already apparent. Pinking her top lip, she sticks her tongue out obscenely. The sight of it, long and livid, always made me scream as she lifted it to reveal double-parked tonsils.

F's in the video too. Usually the cameraman, he looks uncom-fortable being filmed in a green-and-white striped deck chair. The features of his matinée-idol face are coarsening already. He looks shockingly like his twenty-five-year-old brother, sitting next to him, prematurely bloated by drink. Their sunken eyes and mean little mouths are riveting.

When he was blind drunk, lying snoring on the sofa, John used to attach a bluebottle to a stick and shove it up Fuckwit's nostril. 'What are you two wee devils up to?' Maddie asked, giggling. 'It's an experiment we have to do for school,' I'd say.

F is perfect proof that glamour is more than surfaces, it's truly skin deep. His features are handsome, but inside there's something wrong. This once-invisible weakness has forced its way to the surface. It's in his brother's face too. My brother's face is Montgomery Clift's, broken but infinitely spellbinding.

In the mirror — like Kelly in *Naked Kiss* — I promise my own face a better future. Compromise, cowardice, fatty foods, spiritual vertigo, all show in your face. Some are easier to conceal under make-up than others. And yet, the imperfect skin of all those Hollywood heroines dazzled under the key light.

The video is silent so I used ebony-oldie Prince as a soundtrack. Maddie likes Prince, even though he's an off-colour midget; 'It's the tight purple trousers, he really suits them'. I don't know what he's doing these days. One night a few years ago when he was playing Wembley, he picked Lolita up in McDonald's where she was enjoying a supper of slim fries and sweetened orange juice. She's the only girl in town smaller than everybody. He noticed her because she was wearing red tights.

Everyone has their celebrity story. Prince has to dance with somebody. She was always a better dancer than me. I definitely couldn't kiss anyone under five feet.

*   *   *

Suddenly it's four o'clock.

Outside, the sky's changing colour. Bjork's in The Roadhouse eating fruit salad with Greek yoghurt, scribbling in her songbook – the natural face of fame. You notice famous people because they have a look. A communal facial expression that signals their fame. Look at me! Some do it less sickeningly than others.

Wee Lulu's in the Clifton Road video store. Emerging from behind a popcorn stand that comes up to everyone else's waist, she has a big grin you suspect isn't an act. Her big carrot-red hair-do and short stick legs never fail to cheer me up. Someone ought to cast her as Penelope Pitstop.

The guy behind the counter's holding a rabbit. 'Look after the rabbit,' he says to me, when I'd made my selection.

'Just put it down there.'

'It might get run over.'

'Huh?'

'It could run outside into the road. The buses come round that corner faster than diarrhoea.'

'That's the rabbit's problem – I mean, if it's daft enough to run into the road.'

'Give it to me,' Lulu says. Pomposity is the mortal sin of glamour. Wee Lulu's confident but not vain. She understands glamour. Plain women pretending to be clever reject glamour as trivial and not profound. It's worthless because they want it, but think they can't have it with big calves. Lulu, a dwarf, is permanently at risk of becoming dumpy-fat, but stays dead glam. There's no cowardice in her. I'm getting carried away. It's easy to like folk you don't know.

I went back home with *True Romance* and a bottle of Laurent-Perrier. They don't sell half bottles.

Prince was still playing. I had a dance while fast-forwarding through the ads on the video. I love *True Romance*, it's such a jolly film. Quentin Tarantino is an innocent with a sense of humour.

I doubt if I could kiss Quentin Tarantino either. Of course his Neanderthal-chic look doesn't necessarily mean he isn't a sex God. Though even sexy-looking men are sometimes rotten kissers. It's a dilemma I'm never likely to lose sleep over.

The doctor downstairs can't stand my record collection. He's French.

Knock, Knock.
'Who's there?'
'It's the doctor.'
'Dr who?'
'The doctor from downstairs.'
Silence.
'Could you turn the music down?'

Music and drunkenness go together.

I shut Prince up, but upped the volume on the video. Watching the credits, I clenched my eyes shut as I opened the bottle. The pop always makes me jump out of my skin even though I know it's coming. A boyfriend of Irene the Slut's was blinded by a champagne cork. 'It was really exciting,' Maddie told me. 'She had to take him to hospital and everything, but by the time they were finished with him in Ophthalmology, Irene was bored to tears in the waiting room. He got his sight back, but she dumped him.'

The first sip is the jolliest.

Watching the movie, I felt time moving.

Time is of no consequence in Paris or Venice, but means

everything in Tokyo and New York. Killing time, watching a movie in the afternoon is different from watching a movie on a plane, on your way somewhere. In the spring, I'll make up my mind when I'm travelling. Get on that phone and book that ticket. After all, what's seven years between relatives.

The Wrong Man

Movie stars didn't keep their money. They spent what they earned or never earned enough. Marilyn lived in a bourgeois bungalow eating hamburgers. Judy couldn't pay her hospital bills so she booked into The Plaza and ate every dessert on the menu.

There are millions of excuses for spending money. That new pair of crocodile boots, like the pair in the cupboard (only with a higher heel), is always essential to go on living – because you could be dead tomorrow, and never see the credit card bill.

But spending is also a sign of faith in your future. That there's a solution around the corner, a party worth dressing up for, any number of reasons to celebrate. I can fritter away the money Maddie sent for my fare, because I've almost made up my mind not to go. And if I change my mind I can find more money someplace.

This morning my face is marked by innocence. But I'm my father's daughter – I'm not going to work tonight. I've already called the prison with a really good excuse. Fuckwit was always calling in sick while we played drums in the background to aggravate his hangover.

Without the Fun Film Club hanging over me all day, I can

do anything. Right now, my murderers are probably reading on the notice board: SORRY, LADS, MISS WHIPLASH IS SICK. NO MOVIE TONIGHT.

My bathroom window overlooks the rose garden cut into the middle of our mansion block. No one ever goes down there except Old Anna, a woman with a giant pair of scissors she uses to cut the heads off yellow roses. And the gardener, who's addicted to the big tree outside my window. He's always fiddling with the weeds circling its trunk, disturbing the giant magpie that lives in it. If I go out and forget to close the window, I always run to my jewel box when I return to make sure the piece of glass from the mirror I broke is still safe in there. A human wouldn't steal a bit of broken glass but a bird might. We saw a programme about magpies in school, back when the world was all jellies and ice cream. John would know whether or not they collect glass.

Old Anna's out there this morning, but I don't see her scissors. Her Givenchy dressing gown is drooping open, revealing a flesh-toned satin bra, probably Rigby & Peller. 'I'm enjoying the pollution, dear,' she shouted. Waving, I closed the window.

Maddie called at the crack of dawn as I was drinking coffee from a yellow china cup that used to belong to Old Money.

'You'll never guess where I am!'

'Surprise me.'

'Glasgow! I got bored waiting for you. There's no point asking you to come up here. I'm going to fly into London and fetch you on my way back. I've already booked everything so you can't say no.' Her plot's flawless. Not only can she force me to the airport, she can also buy me a travel outfit first.

'When are you coming?' I asked.

'Next Friday,' she said. 'A week today. The thirteenth.'

'I get the message.'

'I'm staying at Devonshire Gardens, you know. Your aunts are sick with jealousy even though they won't admit it. I counted the wrinkles on your Auntie Vagina's dish last night.'

'How many does she have?'

Maddie made a sound like a wounded dog, her version of laughter. 'I lost count! She's got millions around the eyes alone. And that Fat Spam's as fat as ever. Remember that mate of hers – what was she called? Martini?'

'Anytime, anyplace, anywhere.'

'She stole Fat Spam's boyfriend!'

'I didn't know she had one.'

'He wasn't much to look at. Big red nose.'

'Did he shag her?'

'How would I know!'

I heard my post landing.

'I have to go,' I said. 'I'm working today.'

'I thought you only worked at night?' she sounded suspicious. 'That job of yours is weird. And tell that husband of yours I won't take no for an answer this time. It's bad enough that I wasn't invited to the wedding. At this rate I'll be in my coffin before I get a chance to inspect him.'

'He's dying to meet you too.'

'Don't be cheeky. Does he call you Carole or Maria?'

'He calls me Frau.'

'Frau?'

'German for wife.'

'Hmm,' she said. 'I might have known. I named you after Carole Lombard.'

'I know. The screwball comedienne who died in a plane crash.'

'Considered good looking,' Maddie said. 'I really wish you would do something about that hair of yours.'

'I have to go.'

'Are you still at that praying? Remember when you were wee, you were never off your knees. What on earth did you and God have to gossip about?'

'There's someone at my door.'

'I know when I'm not wanted,' she said. 'I'll be seeing you.'

There's an invitation to a medical experiment waiting on the white carpet in the hall.

Would you, the yellow leaflet asks, be prepared to swallow a very small tube?

It's great when you wander into an expensive shop and see nothing you want to buy! This afternoon in Bond Street, after my facial, I examined the shoddy hemline of a puke-coloured dress, held badly cut leather jeans against myself – no need for a mirror, I wouldn't steal those if you paid me. Designers must get a right laugh at the old bags who can afford them.

I used to feel an obligation to steal something now and again, to prove I hadn't lost my nerve. Now I've given up bourgeois habits like boasting about shoplifting.

The rain started as I was walking home. The sight of my shiny black boots traversing puddles passed the time as I walked up Edgware Road, aware of the sleazy street stretching straight ahead. Soon I'd have to cross the Westway by tunnel. I'm too lazy to detour into the quieter territory of council estates and office sandwiches. But I love rain, depend on it to cleanse body odour off the city.

Outside the post office where I used to cash my cheques a girl with superwaif legs wearing a sweatshirt with high-cut cyclamen knickers, holding a crutch, was trying to scream her way to the front of the payphone queue. Her fair short hair was stuck to her skull. Just a little touch of lipstick, dear, you'd be lovely. Who does she want to call? I have a feeling he's not home.

We made eye contact. She glanced at my glossy mahogany walking-stick. I've never hit anyone over the head with it. One day on the train I cracked it accidentally on purpose into a pinstripe's shins. But that was ages ago, when the wound was fresh. Poison oozed from the open toe on to its vacuum-packed dressing, giving the nurses plenty to tut over when they changed it for me twice a week in ward seven.

Irish Rachel came running out of The Roadhouse when she saw me at the zebra. 'He's not in,' she said, 'come and have a seafood pasta.' The London Irish are twice as likely to do themselves in as the London English. I'm always being accused of being Irish, because of my Celtic colouring and odd accent.

She's been feeding me for months because I loaned her a video, and she enjoys cheating the owner – one of those guys with a multi-coloured moustache that clashes with his eyebrows. I know the menu by heart. The pasta sauce is too creamy, it blocks my nose. Nothing like as good as the red wine and garlic sauce I concoct in my own kitchen, but I can't hurt Rachel's feelings. And I like swallowing espresso after espresso, staring at the petroleum canal, thinking about suicide. There's a suicide in England every two minutes. And that's good news for God and population control and funeral parlours. What's the point of mortal sin if no one commits it? Suicide, Al Alvarez says, is a short cut to dying.

Men enjoy strangling themselves, women prefer pills. The report says nothing about jumping off buildings, an increasingly popular method these days favoured by orientals. John was a trend setter for the new breed of Fu Manchus and Mother Ginslings with their bandaged feet and opium dreams.

I couldn't take pills. You have to swallow them gulp by gulp, risking brain damage and kidney failure. You die with the horrible thought that someone is going to meddle with your corpse. You could even be rescued and forced to swallow a tube.

Hanging is a dirty way of dying favoured by perverts. Opening a vein is harder than it looks on TV, even when you're sawing in the right direction. If you jump off a bridge you can be eaten alive by evil big fish. An aggressive splat to be scrubbed off the road is a more dignified death. Certain, courageous. All I would have to do is go up on a roof and wait for vertigo to lure me off the edge. But I can't. Everyone would think I was copying John!

Anyway, why would I want to kill myself?

I ate a third of the pasta, drank a glass of their off-putting cidery sparkling wine and three coffees. Every fortune teller I have ever consulted has promised me three children. Well. I'm not planning to deform my body with childbirth or destroy my soul by devoting my existence to someone else's ka-ka. Babies are sinister. They lie there brainless or fix you with the cold blue gaze of manipulation.

Outside, Sadie the Slink is crossing the zebra with her wee boy. I love two-year-olds! Unfortunately they grow up to be teenagers.

There's another report on the radio about the death of the IRA.

'There's little enough passion in London as it is,' Rachel said. 'What are we going to do without the threat of bombs?'

'It'll be like Berlin without its wall,' I agreed.

'Hey,' Rachel said, opening a bottle of red wine to let it breathe. 'Fancy a cheesecake?' As she tugged the corkscrew, I couldn't resist staring at the veins standing out on her inner arm. Hidden in her chest her heart is beating, pumping blood, capable of bleeding.

'I have to go to work.' I'm an excellent liar. I couldn't force down the cake if she paid me. The owner's wife makes it with impure ingredients. The floozy doesn't even bother to scour her fingernails when she appears in public; what chance do the baking bowls have?

'She works in the Scrubs,' Rachel said to an old geezer paying his bill. She set the bottle of wine down dangerously close to her elbow. 'Shows movies to a bunch of psychos!' He smiled apologetically at me, dropping a pound in the tip saucer. 'Used to be an actress.'

'What did you act in?' he asked.

'Home movies.'

'She's a card, isn't she? What was the name of that advert you were in?'

'It didn't have a name.'

'Remember that one with the fruit and nuts?' she asked the old guy. He nodded. I could tell he was none the wiser. 'What was it again – chocolate or cereal?' she asked, dunking some wine into a glass stained with the dregs of London limescale.

'It was years ago.'

'I recognized her the first time she came in here,' she told the old geezer proudly. Rachel must have been mixing me up with someone else. Everybody looks like someone. My mistake was admitting to my absurd job as an extra in ads. Now she never shuts up about it.

'Wish I had an interesting life.' She sighed, her fingers clutching the goblet of room temperature blood by its neck. 'I suppose I could change my name to Raquel and buy a Wonderbra.' The old guy's laughter was forced. He disappeared into the communal toilet. Rachel delivered the glass of red wine to a woman with a French manicure and a heart-wrenching smile. 'You'll never guess who came in here the other day?'

'Lulu?'

'No, Marianne Faithfull! I nearly died.' Fame has that effect on people, even if it's a celeb they're not in love with.

'Her ex-husband lives above the bank.'

'You're kidding! How do you know?'

'I went to a party in his place by mistake and she was draped across the sofa wearing that bronze satin suit she sings in on TV. I think she bought it in Brown's.'

'Did she look good in it?'

'The suit was slinky. Only her hair was in a pony tail.' Marianne had stood up, a cool glass of white wine in her hand, and murmured, 'Anyone want to hear my new record?' After a gap, Dangerous said, 'We'd love to hear it.' But Marianne went all shy. She sat down. Soon after, we left. As we crossed the road back to our building I could feel dirty drops of rain frizz my hair. I love rain, especially in the dark; and regretted not hearing the record. First thing next morning, I put *Strange Weather* on. Marianne's is just the sort of thrilling, melancholic voice that goes with melon and espresso.

'You actresses all stick together,' Rachel said.

The old geezer and me left together.

'What kind of movies do you show?' he asked.

'Violent ones.'

'What was the last one you showed?'

'*Reservoir Dogs.*'

'Is that allowed?'

'Nobody notices.'

'Can I drive you somewhere?'

'Somewhere?' He blushed, puzzling me. When I was young I wanted to be a celibate Parisian prostitute in red high heels, but it seems unlikely that this old geezer with a face like a fried egg could imagine he's my type.

'We could have a drink,' he said, desperation ascending behind his hectors.

'I just had one, thank you,' I said, dashing into the traffic. I've become more polite than I need to be. It only encourages fuckwits. 'Go fuck yourself with a banana!' I used to scream at anyone who so much as looked at me. But, working in the prison, I get most of my hysteria out at the Fun Film Club playing the part of Miss Whiplash. Now I can't be bothered shouting verbal abuse in the street.

Alex the groovy film-maker boyfriend of slinky Sadie was parking his Jaguar outside my building.

'Hey,' he said. 'Let's drink Absolut Citron then fly backwards in a plane to Australia.' Once when John was digging a hole to Australia, I spotted a centipede. He bashed its brains in with his shovel for me.

'I have a date with a dangerous man,' I said. 'I have to tattoo my lipstick on.' Alex used to pretend not to recognize his wee boy when he saw him in his pushchair, one of those male rivalry things.

The flat felt too calm, as if the furniture had been up to something and just got itself back into place when it heard my key in the door. I opened one of the windows and leaned out, inhaling the damp dramatic yellow roses. Not a bird in sight. A sky with nothing falling out of it.

I looked in my jewel box before taking off my shiny mack and silk shirt and black legs, leaving on my heels and satin bra. I slipped into the fur coat hanging in front of the mirror. A pale forties mink, it used to be Maddie's. She was taller than me until my illness when I lay in bed for a year and grew while her neck shortened with age and sunshine, shrivelling into her body.

'That coat makes me look middle aged,' she'd said on the phone. She had worn it to John's funeral, to keep Jack Frost out. 'I wouldn't be seen dead in it.'

'You're beyond middle age,' I pointed out.

'Cheeky little madam,' she said. 'I'll mail it to you.' I've been planning to wear the mink for ages. Dangerous is scared someone will throw an egg at me. Today I bought a new pair of pale stockings to go with the coat everyone will assume is fake. Black stockings with the strip of flesh not flab at the upper thigh are all I could have imagined wearing when I was given this coat seven years ago. Zelda Fitzgerald was famous in Alabama for her flesh-coloured bathing suit. It clung nudely to her dancer's body, threatening a seductive future. Her brother jumped to his death as well, but madness cheated Zelda out of the suicide that would have suited her. It comforts me to believe she started the fire that burned her to death in the final state sanitarium, a decade after Scott died in Hollywood. The humiliation that hurts like Hell is poverty.

Dangerous telephoned to invite me to a movie.

'I'll meet you there,' he said. 'Don't wear that coat.'

He hung up. Time tricks you when you most expect it. After painting my face and finding something to wear, I would have to wait for ages before going to the cinema.

Suddenly I'm late. I'll have to rush.

*   *   *

Dangerous was waiting outside in his *Breathless* jacket when I jumped out of my cab, head cluttered with muddled conversation.

'You look small tonight,' he said.

'No heels.' Last time I was sick, he fed me vivid cherries, ripe mango, firm figs, and sometimes seven safe small-shelled Scottish oysters. Now that the scar in my toe is clean, I can wear high heels whenever I feel like it.

We bought a salted popcorn to share and took our seat in the front row. We know the ads by heart, it's a struggle finding new movies to see, but we're addicted to the seductive atmosphere of urban cinemas. You know, holding hands in the movie show when all the lights are low.

I've seen this one already; he'd be mad if he knew.

During the movie I left my seat without whispering an excuse and went to the Ladies Room. There were no ladies in there. I had a look in the mirror.

Your nose grows between the ages of thirteen and nineteen. Traffic frightens me. Certainties make it possible to go on living.

I ran the cold tap on my wrists, bought more popcorn to make it look good, and stayed in position for the rest of the movie. Phew. No nervous breakdown tonight. I'm not one of those people who believes in confiding emotional insecurities to the one they love best in all the world. Why should it bother me anyway? I'm not scared to go to the land where the best movies were invented.

Who, me?

Brain

'Death is a kind of pornography at once exciting and unreal.'
Al Alvarez

There's been another plot twist. I should be having lunch with my mother in her Louis-Seize suite at the Ritz. Introducing her to my husband in the privacy of a rented sitting room over-looking Green Park, brain tight with dread at the thought of spending twelve hours on a plane to L.A. with her. Now that I'm older and more idealistic, I can't weird her out with extended silence. I have to be kind. Take an interest. Try not to hurt her feelings. She's paying for my flight. Even though she already paid in advance. The money was spent on shiny forties backache heeled shoes with pink lining and diamanté ankle straps, a satin Prada dress, and a vulgar Cartier watch that's going to be left sulking in the jewel box.

But I'm not demolishing lobster in the Ritz, hearing Maddie tell the story about us staying there when I was wee and being asked to leave because I was roller skating in the corridor. I'm in Glasgow listening to my Judy Garland records. I've been sent to evict my father from the family flat. Judy, who's been locked in my room for years, sings the same song over and over as I wait for F to come in from the pub.

The night is bitter, the stars have lost their glitter.

*   *   *

F knows that his wife, a woman he has spoken to but not seen since she migrated to New Mexico, is in the Royal Infirmary having her heart monitored. Like me, he was informed of her massive coronary in the middle of the night. The hospital contacted him. He's her husband and official next of kin, but not her heir. Maddie telephoned me herself from Intensive Care. Against the advice of the consultant, who 'doesn't have a crystal ball', she predicted authoritatively, 'I'm dying. I won't last the night. I had the full heart attack.'

Before I had the chance to rub the sleep from my eyes, pack my cosmetics, rush to the airport that doesn't open until morning, and ride the rollercoaster shuttle, she continued, 'I'm lying here with wires coming out of me. I know you've never really loved me, but please don't give me a showing up by refusing to come. I'm glad I'm going to die at home.'

It's one of her best performances. I'm proud of her. She'll mention her dead son any minute.

'It's just like you to be living in London at a time like this,' she told me when I arrived next morning with dark circles under my eyes. 'There's no reason why I shouldn't live in my own place now that I've decided to move back here . . . to die. You'll have to tell him.'

I haven't spoken to F for twenty years. The silence wasn't planned. Now I have something to say.

'I can't be stressed,' she added, 'or I'd be happy to tell your father myself.' It was easy to feel sorry for her lying there with no face on, teeth missing at the front, a needle in her arm. Looking at her could have broken my heart. I knew I was only feeling sorry for myself.

'You know, things would have been different between us if he hadn't disgraced the family. The shame of it!' I stared out the window, wishing I was in New York. 'Bearing a child who

74

grows up to take his place among the damned.' She's obviously rehearsed this scene with Vagina. 'Is there something interesting going on out there?' she asked sarcastically. 'I finally force you to visit me and you stand staring into space! I think your aunties want a wee word with you.'

'It's your duty to tell him,' Vagina told me when the sisters had cornered me in the hospital snack bar. 'And I want it done today.'

'You're the forceful one,' Ivy assured me. 'And it's not every day your mother nearly meets her maker.'

'You've always been cheeky,' Vagina added. 'And it was only a matter of time before she came back. Maddie never really fitted in in America.'

Junkie Jenny, a born-again trank addict, cackled in agreement. Someone ought to tell her Valium's dead seventies. And you don't take diazepams during the day, unless you're mixing them with heroin. A Prozac in the morning, a Temazepam at night – that's the ritual for today's unhappy housewife.

'And you're going to inherit everything.' Cousin Fat Spam, daughter of Vagina, said out loud what the others were thinking.

Everything?

'After all she is your mother,' Ivy said. Ivy's three sons – the murderer, the graveyard lurch, and the escapee who married a Greek with an olive oil business – would all turn her into dog ka-ka if it was easy to convert fantasy into reality.

'I practically brought her up,' Vagina said to Ivy, 'and what thanks have I ever got?'

Dangerous kills himself laughing when I tell him that Vagina thinks he should buy her a three-piece suite. 'With all his money,' she says, 'it's the least he can do.' Of course Dangerous isn't rich. He's richer than her. She wants him to buy her a three-piece suite because I was taken to live with her when Maddie went loony.

John went to Ivy's. She beat him on the bare bum with a leather belt she kept swinging from her neck for easy access. 'He's getting the same treatment as my own,' she boasted when visiting Maddie in her private room in the bin. None of the sisters would ever dream that they'd abused their children.

Living with Auntie Vagina and her husband, Uncle Penis, is one of the nightmare flashbacks of my childhood. People's pet names for each other are disgusting. Instead of calling themselves Vagina and Penis like everyone else did behind their back (because she's frigid and he's impotent) they used to coo 'Snucksie' and 'Poopsie' in really loud voices, even though they couldn't stand the sight of each other.

My worst memory is bathnight. Vagina couldn't get her head around the fact that, in my house, you had a bath every night; a shower every morning. You could throw in an extra soaking when you came home from school if you liked. Maddie always encouraged a good thorough scouring at every opportunity.

'I'm not rich like your mum,' Vagina was fond of telling me. Her bathroom had just been put in. 'Not so long ago, it was a tin basin in the kitchen.'

On a Sunday evening at the obscenely early hour of six, Fat Spam and I were expected to climb into the tub together. Vagina, who believes that locking a bathroom door is immoral, would come in to inspect our naked bodies at regular intervals.

'What are you doing standing there?' she'd ask Fat Spam.

'She told me to wait until she was done.'

'Do you have to do what she tells you?'

'Yes.'

'You're older than her!' Vagina shrieked, shoving her big-bummed daughter into the scalding water as I jumped out. Even in those days, Spam habitually had her nose in a magazine seeking infallible advice on how to get a man.

After Spam had pretended to wash herself, Auntie Vagina climbed into the suds. Uncle Penis used the water last, somehow managing to extract a thrill from the fact that it was lukewarm and dirty. 'Water was cold tonight,' he'd say, coming into the big room in his bobbly pyjamas, 'because you lot used it first.'

When we visited Maddie in the bin, Vagina said, 'It's no' right, Madeleine. We've just had our bath put in and the wee one wants to wear it out.'

Maddie was propped up in bed wearing a pukey sugar-pink négligé, blowing smoke over the scarlet roses F had sent her. She went crazy if anyone brought her white flowers. 'The Chinese think white is unlucky,' she cried, doing her best to live up to her crazy image.

F has been ordered not to visit her in hospital this time either.

'The embarrassment of having to face him may kill her,' Vagina said.

'He looks terrible,' Ivy agreed.

'Of course you can't blame us,' Vagina explained, 'we didn't marry him, Maddie did.' Believe it or not, they wanted to marry him. He was the Paul Newman of the East End when he was young.

The moon grows colder, and suddenly you're older.

Judy's voice echoes around the flat at the top of the smoke-blackened East End building. The sisters were born here and have lived in it all their lives. At any time after Maddie inherited it, we could have moved somewhere else. We could have gone to the West End, if we liked, or even bought a big detached house. I'm glad we moved upstairs into this flat when Old Money died. Maybe I'll move back here some day and sit at the bay window watching the traffic.

When I escaped to New York, I was always afraid to open my hotel window. That proves I had vertigo all along. John visited. He bought his own ticket. When we were alone he told me his plans. He'd decided to walk across America, a flask of water prepared for crossing the desert, all the way to California.

'What will you do when you get there?'

'Walk back again.' He was hoping I'd volunteer to go with him.

When anyone else was in the room, he sat in the corner impersonating a cat.

'Your brother's weird,' the film-school chums told me. Underneath, I hated them. He was always going to be my best friend. I was glad when he left.

When we were young we were always sitting around in the dark, shining torches to break the monotony, chattering about New York. The cinematic city is even more like a movie in real life than it is in *Mean Streets* and *Taxi Driver* and *New York, New York*.

'We won't live in a hotel when we go there,' he'd said. 'We'll sleep under a bush in Central Park.'

'What if somebody kills us?'

'We'll have the cloak of invisibility.'

I'd wanted to live in the Algonquin Hotel, having champagne cocktails sent to my bath. Dorothy Parker's 'Résumé' would be superglued to the tiles above the marble tub.

> Razors pain you;
> Rivers are damp;

Acids stain you;
And drugs cause cramp.
Guns aren't lawful;
Nooses give;
Gas smells awful;
You might as well live.

But Maddie had booked me into an anonymous Murray Hill hotel with dusty mirrors and excellent security. Already terrified of traffic, every day I passed The Factory walking all the way downtown to NYU, the soles of my sandalled feet raw and dirty.

'When you see your aunties, you won't mention that other thing?'

'What other thing?'

'You know,' she whispered stagily, 'the tubercular toe.' She had begged me to keep my illness quiet, even paid me to make up an explanation for my walking stick.

'I fired my doctor for calling it that.'

'Consumption then,' she said. 'Your aunties wouldn't understand. It's dirty folk that get it.'

'What about Grandfather's wife?'

'That was in the olden days! Everybody had it then.'

Before the week was out Maddie was her old self again, off the drip, sitting up in bed chewing low-fat toffees.

'What do you think of the new shade?' she asked, pursing her lips. She's into browns these days, which is an improvement on pink.

'Lovely,' I said. 'Don't talk with your mouth full.'

'I nearly broke my back lifting her for a blanket bath this

morning,' her nurse said to me as if Maddie wasn't there.

'Don't you have a bedpan to empty somewhere?' I said.

Maddie giggled. These days she enjoys my cheek. While the woman was definitely still in earshot, Maddie said, 'See her, she's a dead ringer for a lesbian, that one.' The nurse does bear a striking resemblance to Hattie Jacques in *Carry On Doctor* – but isn't she a man-eater? Never argue with an invalid.

'I definitely had the full heart attack,' Maddie told me for the millionth time. 'The consultant told me. Very nice man. Wouldn't you like to have married a doctor?'

'I hate doctors.'

'You would. You could even have been a doctor, with that big brain of yours. I don't understand you.'

She's inspected Dangerous Donald. He's not a doctor, but he's winning her over with his boyish charm. 'Looks nothing like your brother,' she said to me when he walked in, satisfied with his blond hair and expensive suit. And to him, 'Thank God you're not going to force me to become a grannie.'

'My mother died of heart failure too.'

'And two of your lovely sisters.' She looked terrified.

'They were fat.'

'Everyone dies of heart failure.' The heart stops. You see the face of God. Is he smiling? I used to imagine God as the spitting image of Grandfather. He had the obvious bony face, the straggly white hair, and, instead of Grandfather's selfish blue eyes, a sage's strong grey eyes with surprisingly long lashes. Now when I think of God He's Cary Grant, charming and blank; giving everything.

'It will be your turn next,' she said. 'But you can't say no to me, not when I'm dying. I need my flat back. He's lived there rent free for years!'

'I've said I'll see him.'

'Think of all the things I did for you when you were wee,' she said.

'Don't push your luck.'

Yesterday I realized, as I buzzed the entryphone, that it would be easier to break the news if I could offer alternative accommodation. But the supply of tenements is used up. The flats left in this building are occupied by sisters and cousins who wouldn't want to share with F. Maddie's not rich, as she frequently reminds me, and even if she were – why should she spend my inheritance rehousing him?

'I've lived with the guilt,' she told me yesterday, 'and now I'm being paid back for my father's generosity.'

My father will not be leaving me money in his will. He doesn't have one. His eyes are yellow. He drinks. He has no friends. Nobody loves him. Even his mother, ancient and incarcerated in an insane asylum, refuses to acknowledge him.

I have bad news for this man. I'm going to make him homeless. Dangerous is suspicious of people who boast about being moral. Christians are nice to you so that you'll be nice back. Parents look after you when you're young so that you'll grow up and be their insurance policy.

If it's a repayment plan, do you only have to be kind to the one who bought you all the toys? Or can you choose randomly, do your wee bit of good and get it over with, then indulge a spell of selfishness?

How do choices become so simple – how do people know for sure that fighting for an unhappy calf is more moral than sticking up for a carrot. *Hey, that carrot's bored to death stuck in the ground all day, then some vegetarian bastard comes along and chomps it!* '

Can anyone prove that a video doesn't feel sad when you don't rent it? Hurting a tape's feelings could be just as bad as evicting your dad. God should really give us more of a clue. All this guesswork can wear you out. No wonder morality's become another copycat affair.

But I'm in luck. F's not in. Either that or, like me, he doesn't answer the doorbell. I ran back down the dusty stairs, glancing out the landing window. There was no washing hanging out. Maddie used to say, 'I'm mortified every time the neighbours see your Auntie Dolly's knickers.' There are too many underwear thieves these days to hang lace basques on the line. And Auntie Dolly's dead. Vagina and Ivy and Jenny all buy their pants in M&S; white cotton, large, suitable for the tumble dryer.

I passed their doors quietly, convinced someone was watching me through Junkie Jenny's spy hole. She munches Valium all day, then lurches in dark hallways waiting for something to happen. Her doctor ought to tell her about Prozac, I have enough on my plate. Of course Valium controls her cackling, and at least she doesn't stick her oar into other people's business.

'Not in?' Dangerous asked, as I climbed into the passenger seat of Maddie's hired blue Mercedes. It matches his eyes. He hasn't met his father-in-law before. We decided it was for the best for him to wait outside.

'We'll have to come back later,' I said.

A woman wearing a cherry coat stared in the windscreen at me as we sat wondering where to go to kill time. Her face, a different shade of red to the coat, is uncomfortably familiar. Does she know me? Or is she just a nosy tart.

Dangerous started up the car. As we drove off, the red woman hesitated before walking away.

*　　*　　*

Driving back to the hospital, I shouted, 'There's Grandfather's hotel!'

It looked enormous when I was wee, and still does. A line of tramps was heading for it, progressing along Duke Street in the Chinese fashion.

'I thought that had been sold too?'

'It's been turned into a hostel for down and outs. We could send Fuckwit there.'

'You couldn't!' he said, laughing. 'Your own father?'

'The Great Western or Great Eastern or something it's called now.'

'Isn't that the hotel in *Twin Peaks*?'

'Probably.' F doesn't watch TV. He hasn't the patience. He's not likely to have heard of *Twin Peaks*.

'Why is he called Fuckwit anyway?'

'It suits him.'

'What's his real name?'

'John, I think.'

Back at her cluttered bedside, I asked Maddie, 'Is Mad Moira still alive?'

'Mad Moira,' she scoffed. 'How would I know!' And then, 'Why wouldn't she be alive? You should be worrying about your own mother and not Mad Moira.'

Mad Moira the cinema usherette sneaked me into the first movie I saw alone in a cinema.

The first movie I'd seen in a cinema was *The Sound of Music* when I was really wee. I'm mortified to admit that I enjoyed it so much I wanted to stay in and see it again.

'Can we?' I asked, face full of glee. 'Can we just sit here and wait for it to happen again?'

'We'll come back next week,' Maddie said.

John tugged at my hand but I wouldn't move out of my seat. Eventually she lifted me up and carried me into the foyer.

'I'd like one of they ice creams,' I said sneakily.

Standing in the queue, she set me down. While she was distracted paying for the 99s, I started shrieking, 'Help! This woman is not my mummy!' John joined in.

People shook their heads, shocked. Maddie went red. It didn't look good for her. 'The wee one's a card,' she said. That didn't stop the manager being brought in, or the police being called – just in case.

'Can you actually prove these children are yours?' the manager asked, while we were locked in his office waiting for the police to arrive.

'They don't look a bit like you,' the usherette said.

Maddie started to cry. The Lana Turner eye make-up was running all over her rouged cheeks. 'I was only kidding,' I said. 'She's our mum.' The big people looked at me suspiciously.

'Are you sure?' the manager asked.

In Mad Moira's cinema, the movies were racier.

'Nobody's watching the fillum,' she told me, before making her famous noise, 'Eeegh.' And warning me, 'Never go near the toilets, no matter how desperate you are.'

'It's unnatural,' Maddie said. 'A woman that age taking an interest in you. Her face is plastered in muck from Woolie's too.'

Moira lived in the next close to us. She had a kitchen with a bed in it and no inside toilet. She loved to repeat the story about the time she was shining her torch on the front row, looking for wankers, when she realized one of them was a corpse. 'Eeegh!' She enjoyed repeating this so much she could hardly get out her punchline: 'The movie wasn't that bad.'

Sometimes I knocked on her door at five and she wasn't even dressed. 'Can you get me in tonight?' I asked.

'Wait at the fire exit at nine,' she always replied. The big feature was about to start. She pretended to be going to stock up on choc ices while her boss's attention was distracted. Sometimes, she even had to eat the ices in her tray to make it look good.

'Mad Moira's cinema isn't there any more,' Maddie said.

'I know.'

'Did you drive past it?'

'You told me yesterday. It's a wee brain transplant you need, not a pacemaker.'

The Rio had been demolished years ago. There's still a big hole in the ground where it used to be. This gap is much more exciting than a bingo hall.

'Don't think,' Maddie assured me, 'that I had this heart attack to get out of taking you on that holiday. We'll go to Hollywood when I'm better. The only change of plan will be that afterwards we'll fly back again together instead of saying goodbye in L.A.'

'Great,' I said.

'I'll swing for you. Do you want a toffee?'

'I never eat toffee.'

'You'll need to get over these food fads of yours.' She hesitated. 'You know El Dorado isn't your scene, don't you? My house wouldn't suit you. It was a great idea of mine to put you up in a hotel. You always liked hotels. Anyway, I'm selling that place now.'

I didn't bother pointing out that she always put the sisters up in hotels too – admittedly less expensive hotels. No one has been to her famous house, though Vagina's determined 'to get to the bottom of Maddie's secret'.

'Have you busted up with Jonathan then?'

'He's never lived in my house in his life!'

'Nobody said he lives there.'

'I hardly know the man.'

'Is he still in the suntan lotion business?'

'You know he retired years ago. Where's that husband of yours anyway?'

'He's gone to pack.' We're using her suite in Devonshire Gardens. The dark-damson bed blacks out everything at night but during the day the room's too dark. I'm blind as a bat until I go into the bright bathroom.

'What? Leaving already!'

'We're selling our place at the seaside.'

'I never had trouble selling a place in my life. So you're staying on?' I glared at her. She made the coarse laughing noise. 'You wouldn't desert me, would you?'

Vagina came in with a bag of withered apples.

'Cox's Pips,' she said.

'Big spender,' Maddie sneered. There was an astonishing clip of Shirley Bassey on mid-morning telly the other day. Wearing a piece of gauze that couldn't conceal her sagging beezers or spare tyre, she made a right meal out of 'Big Spender'. Her passion made it glamorous. She lives in Cannes nowadays – or is it Monaco? She could have been walking on the beach with Graham Greene, or neighbours with Grace Kelly. Now they're dead, she can live in either sun city without bumping into them.

'The wee one looks exactly the same,' Vagina said, eyeing my intellectual chic *Funny Face* existential polo and flat Parisian soft leather ballet shoes disapprovingly. 'Seen your father yet?'

'He wasn't in.'

'You mean you went to see him without knocking on my door?! You could have brought that husband of yours in for a cup of tea.'

'She must have heard you wring your tea bags out and use them again,' Maddie said. 'Her husband's dead glamorous. Really brainy looking. What's the name of that film with the guy that looks like him in it?'

'*The Moderns.*'

'We're not all rich like you,' Vagina said. 'I can only afford one box of tea bags a week.'

'Haven't seen it,' Maddie said. 'And I don't expect your auntie has either. Who is it that looks like him again?'

'Keith Carradine.' I only love him in that movie. He's a painter in Paris who leaves for Hollywood at the end. You have to be really pure to keep loving the same hero.

'Never heard of him.' His vulnerability is clean. It shows in his face that he's strong enough to be hurt. Looking at him reminds me of Montgomery Clift's car crash. You can't destroy a great face no matter how hard you try.

'And somebody dead famous says he's got the charm of a young Frank Sinatra,' Maddie insisted.

'Frank Sinatra's horrible looking!' Vagina shrieked triumphantly.

'Looks and charm are two different things,' Maddie said, rolling her eyebrows. 'Who was it that said it again?'

'Shena Mackay.'

'Who?' Vagina doubled her chin into her neck in disgust.

'She's a woman around your age only she doesn't have a double chin.'

'Cheeky devil! Did he have an affair with her?'

'I don't think so.'

'My God!' Vagina shouted. 'Has it been going on your whole married life?'

'Is this true?' Maddie asked, alarmed.

'Don't be ridiculous. She's just a writer he sat next to at dinner once ages ago.'

'Is she blonde or dark?'

'It's irrelevant,' I said. Neither of them looked convinced.

Silence forced our three sets of eyes to drift to the TV which Maddie keeps on with the sound down at all times. 'A telly's your best friend at my age,' she said lasciviously. 'That Judith Chalmers is a nice-looking woman.'

'It's Gloria Hunniford,' Vagina retorted, digging her chin into her neck.

'Where would I be without my telly?' Maddie asked.

'Search me,' I said. But I'm my mother's daughter. I still miss those American soaps from my teenage years. Some mornings I wake up and wonder what happened to the guy with the perm in *One Life to Live* — or was it *All My Children*? Men with perms and wee frumpy false women with orange tans are the lifeblood of soaps. Daytime TV is a soap without a plot, a gathering of chatterboxes with nothing to say.

'Have you had any children yet?' Vagina asked. 'A marriage without children is a sin.'

'Oh dry up,' Maddie said. 'You're up a bum tree. That daughter of yours doesn't even have a man! You should have kicked her out years ago.' Vagina was flabbergasted. Maddie usually pretends to agree with her.

'I know you're not well,' she said. 'I'm not going to lower myself to argue with you.'

'Fat Spam's about forty,' Maddie said for my benefit, 'and she still lives at home!'

'I know,' I said.

'Do you remember when you were wee, folk used to think she was your mother and I was your sister?'

'No.'

'You do so!'

'I remember everyone thought me and John were twins.' Vagina crossed herself.

'I'm sick hearing about him,' Maddie said. We never talk about him. At this time of year, I dream about him.

'That brother of yours was almost the death of me. Where do you think you're going?'

'Running off with a Chinaman.'

'If you're going to the toilet,' she shouted after me, 'make sure your bum doesn't touch the seat!'

I wasn't tempted to disobey her order, the hospital's toilets were filthy. The glamour of being pale, frail and dangerous to breathe in is ruined when confronted with the reality of NHS germs.

The cracked plastic seat was lolling at a slovenly angle, exposing enamel that stank of woman waste. Standing up, it seemed to take for ever. At least my inner thigh muscles were being toned. I was bored to tears waiting for it to finish. It was lonely being in there all by myself yet the presence of a stranger in the next cubicle would have disturbed me. Visiting a toilet with someone you know is the end. If a smell wafts from their cubicle under the partition into yours, you can never look them in the eye again.

As I dried my hands with a coarse green paper towel, I smelled my knuckles and indulged a brief fantasy about machine-gunning Maddie. John used to be in a gun club. He kept his pistol under my bed. Where do people go when they die? His soul could be in China. Or walking about in Tokyo maybe, thinking of me.

He could be haunting Hollywood, or asleep in Heaven. Or sipping iced tea with Cary Grant. Would they use straws? I doubt it. The iced tea in this country is foul. New York City is the venue for iced tea. I ripped a dead piece of skin off my bottom lip then covered the tear with Chanel 36.

Vagina had been replaced by the consultant when I returned.

'Mr Blur, this is my daughter. She used to have long hair.' A sleaze-bag with big ears and an arrogant stoop looked me up and down. His name's on his coat in case he forgets it. Reluctantly I made eye contact. His small eyes twinkled perversely.

'I can see the resemblance. Your mother's had a narrow escape.' I picked up her magazine, flicking. It's full of faces you'd love to punch.

'She'd be more like me if she was blonde. You know,' Maddie confided, 'she could have been a doctor. Threw her life away going to acting school then getting sick.'

'An actress?' Mr Blur looked dubious. Probably nervous I'd want a free medical opinion about some imaginary palpitation. Actors are all neurotic.

'Not likely,' Maddie said. 'When she finally did get a part in a movie she didn't want it! Too old now of course.' The thought of all that supervised snogging gave me a breakdown. I wanted not to be in movies but old movies where the lips press but there are no tongues.

'Jolly good,' Mr Blur said, lurching off to his next victim.

'You could have given him a wee smile at least.'

'Are you my mum or a pimp for geriatrics?'

'Cheeky bissum,' she said, face screwed up in disgust.

Vagina returned from the hospital shop with a bunch of floppy daffs.

'What's she been saying about me?'

Maddie turned her nose up at the flowers. 'I'm taking a nap.'

I offered to drive Vagina home. 'Thanks very much,' she said, 'I'll take the bus.' I shrugged. 'The bus has always been good enough for the likes of me,' she boasted, patting her regulation crash-helmet hair-do.

Driving Dangerous to the airport early this morning, he asked me, 'What were you scared of when you were wee?'

'Nothing.' I was concentrating on the road, flat and safe and empty, occasionally seeing Maddie's Honey Honey on my lips in the rearview. Wearing scarlet first thing makes you look like you've been up all night drinking whisky, inappropriate for a dawn kiss.

'I hated fresh cream,' he said. 'It's terrifying the way it just sits in the middle of meringues managing not to fall out.'

'I was one of those wee girls who jumped off roofs because I was told not to.' I saved all my fears for when I was big.

'What roof did you jump from?'

'The school shed. We shouted, "Diplodocus is coming!" then jumped on to the grass.'

'Did you ever break a leg?'

'No. My friend broke her wrist.' I wonder if the join shows when Lolita raises her arm to the Soho spotlight. 'It didn't knit properly. Maddie said it was because she doesn't eat enough greens, her bones are low-class.'

Dangerous laughed.

I pulled up in front of the automatic doors. John and me used to run through them then jump back out again before they closed.

'For God's sake stop playing with that door,' Maddie said,

'we'll miss our plane!' We were always ages early and had to spend a fortune in the Duty Free after waving goodbye to F and John. 'Off on your travels again,' F used to say to his spend, spend, sunbathe wife.

'Flying's dead glamorous,' she replied.

Dangerous jumped out of the car and said, 'Give up guilt for Lent.'

'Every time you leave me for a minute it feels like goodbye,' I said in my early-period Liz Taylor voice.

'It's because you can't live without me.'

After watching him rush inside the terminal, I parked the car and waited long enough for him to have disappeared into the sky.

I couldn't resist a look inside my favourite airport. And I needed to prepare myself with espresso for the drive back. The traffic's going to be worse on the return journey and I'm useless without a sane audience in the passenger seat.

I had to have a gin and tonic with my coffee. On the flight up, I was given a plastic glass of blue gin with flat tonic. I still can't get over it! Usually airlines supply excellent mixers. Gin without fizz is like a movie with the lights on. A perfect sparkly icy gin in the sixties leather lounge helped to destroy the memory of that imperfect drink. But I could never be a gin hound! The stink, the bourgeois tint to the bottle, and its reputation as a weeping woman's drink puts me off. Nothing beats the purity of vodka. Even the word is exciting and clean.

F took us to the airport to wave at the planes as one of our treats when Maddie went insane. I sulked, unable to see the point of it. 'Planes are for flying off in,' I said, crushing him.

Maddie was always rubbing it in that he was never invited abroad.

Now I adore airports not because of their associations but their atmosphere. There's a tension in the travellers, as if everyone's about to go insane or be resurrected. The purgatorial potential of expectation and disappointment can be scraped off the air, even in a small departure lounge like this one.

I was on my third espresso, watching a woman with Spanish legs out of the corner of my eye. She's definitely travelling back into the sun today. The edges of her chocolate eyes are cracking already in anticipation as she wraps the skinny fishnet pins around each other. She'll change on to a bigger plane at Heathrow. She could be murdered by the end of the day.

I have the key to F's flat in my shiny black bag with the long handles and security stud. 'He never answers the door, you have to let yourself in.'

I've started to think of it as F's flat, even though it's Maddie's flat, and is still referred to as 'Old Money's flat'. It's become F's flat because he's being kicked out of it.

'We're running out of time,' she told me last night. 'You have to tell him today come Hell or high water. I'm getting out of here next week and I can't exist in a hotel for long in this condition.' She sighed. 'There's decorators to organize. Builders. Do you think I should have one bathroom or two? You never know, at my age. When are you going to see him?'

'Tomorrow. I tried to see him today.' I phoned him yesterday, but hung up when he answered. His voice disturbs me the way his face used to. When we were in the same room, I trained my eyes to avoid his corner. Maddie had allocated him a chair. He wasn't allowed to sit on the good leather Chesterfield. Sometimes I sneaked a look while he was absorbed in his beer. John and I didn't really hang around the living room. We were up on the roof, in the kaff downstairs, locked in my room – plotting the future.

'That place is going to be transformed. It shouldn't be difficult for you to get rid of him,' she said, not looking at me. 'One thing's for sure, I need double-glazing. The noise from that road is ridiculous. What colour should we make the big room? You hated his guts when you were wee. Remember what you used to call him?'

Fuckwit used to be a smoothie – one of those men in the seventies who wore a sports jacket, drove Maddie's convertible (in the days when she was feminine and didn't drive), and had hair that looked dyed. F didn't dye his hair but used bottled grease to achieve the fake effect.

The day Maddie went insane he met me and John at the school gates.

'Who's the smoothie?' Lolita asked. She'd been to our place millions of times and never met him.

'He's John's dad,' I said.

'Your dad,' John said.

'He's a hot banana,' Lolita said. 'Can I sniff through his underwear drawer?'

'You're perverse.'

'Get in the car,' F said, the habitual puzzled look on his fattening face.

'There isn't room for all of us.' He was mortified by the white Rolls Royce she'd bought him and never took it out of the garage. You have to sympathize, everyone would have thought he was fucking Gary Glitter.

'Squeeze in,' he suggested.

'I could sit on John's knee,' Lolita offered.

'You can take the bus,' I said.

'You're not being very nice to your friend,' F said. She simpered at him.

'She lives nowhere near us.' John and I climbed into the passenger seat of the futuristic Ferrari. He slammed the door in her face.

'Why have you come to meet us anyway?'

'Your mother is sick.'

'Again.'

'She's in hospital.'

John stared straight ahead, making driving noises.

'Which one?'

'Sacred Heart,' he muttered.

'Yikes,' I said. 'She's lost the banana then?'

'She's . . . not well.'

'Mental,' I said to John.

'Bonkers,' he agreed.

'Not all there,' I added.

'Mad as a halfwit,' he said.

'Stop it you two.'

'Do you think she'll do herself in?' It's a well-known fact that I'm going to inherit everything.

But the Sacred Heart was the making of Maddie. She got a really good psychiatrist, who drummed it into her that she could do anything, go anywhere – with her money. The seeds of escape were sown long before John provided the motivation to get on that plane heading for her place in the sun.

*　　*　　*

It was lunchtime when I got here. I rang the bell three times, our family code, then let myself in with the spare key.

I expected to find him passed out in the living room, but he surprised me by not being in. Going straight into my room, I put Judy Garland on to cheer things up.

Even though my door's been locked for seven years, there isn't a smell. My room, which used to be Grandfather's, is still white and perfect and new-looking. I'm sitting on the carpet, watching Marilyn Monroe in the mirrored wall. Pasted on to the big poster of her in her *Gentlemen Prefer Blondes* outfit, there's a small pic of Sylvia Plath from the peroxide summer. Sylvia looks pleased with herself. She's just enjoyed her first breakdown. Next to her, Ian Curtis exposes his soul. No sign of Sid Vicious, thank God.

Ambiguity surrounds their suicides. Did they mean to die or attract more attention? Immortality is always intentional. Each of them is famous for failure.

In a silver frame on the dressing table, there's the famous picture of Louise Brooks holding a long string of twenties pearls. Not only suicides, but self-destructive artists complete the reflection in the dark mirror of the glamour cult. Brooksie's beauty seems inviolable, encased in black-and-white geometry. But she lived for years alone in a squalid New York hotel writing *Lulu in Hollywood*, becoming ugly, before being banished to Rochester to play her final role as ravished eccentric alcoholic. It's shocking to realize, when watching a video of *Pandora's Box*, that the clear-cut Louise has no waist. From the back, she's a rectangle. The lines of her perfect hair-do framing her unanswerable bone structure distract your attention from her fat back.

Some laugh. These pictures should be John's. Fancy them being in my room. The panic of spiritual vertigo is written all over my face.

Like Vagina said yesterday, 'The wee one looks exactly the same.' The sisters have been saying that for years.

'Not changed a bit.'

'Hard as nails.'

'Dead ruthless.'

'Cheeky wee midden.'

And I've been taken in, believing that I don't have a self-destructive bone in my body. And this eternity of certainty is exhausting. Especially when pomposity is a mortal sin. And I haven't given up. I'm still secretly hoping God will reward me. For still being alive?

Judy's singing: *The dreams you dreamed have all gone astray.*

Even F's key in the lock sounds nervous.

Does he know I'm here?

That great beginning, has seen a final ending.

The door shuts behind him. He's in the hallway.

I can see him. He hasn't noticed me. He looks of course nothing like the man in the video he sent but somehow shockingly manages to resemble me.

Good riddance. Goodbye.
Every trick of his you're on to.

Pity will ruin me now.

But fools will be fools
And where's he gone to?

He hasn't noticed my open door. The music doesn't intrigue him. Maybe he was listening to the radio before he went out, maybe not. He's gone straight into the big room to lie down. The swanky sofa's in front of the window so that he can keep an eye on the road.

'Your brother might've been saved,' he told me. 'If he hadn't fallen into that traffic.'

Oh no, I don't think so.

The world gets rougher. It's lonelier and tougher.

Tiptoeing into the hallway, I could run away now. I have time to get out. He's opening a bottle.

Oh no, he's finally aware of the music. He's trying to figure out where it's coming from.

Ever since this world began
There's nothing sadder than
A one-man woman
Looking for
the man
that got
away.

He's in the doorway. He's seen me. Exhaustion is etched on top of illness on his fat face. Layer upon layer of decay, it can never be scraped clean. His hangdog eyes are hopeful and dismayed. Surprises for him are never good, but he can't get out of the habit of wanting them to be.

Instinctively, I resort to my old habit of focusing beyond him. I appear to be looking at him, but it's the door frame I'm examining. I haven't rehearsed my lines. I haven't a clue what the script is. But even when you don't lift a finger to prepare for an intolerable situation, one presents itself anyway. Suddenly, saving the day, I remembered the time me and Lolita saw him urinating in the sink.

'Fuck,' she said, 'look at the Smoothie's plonker!'

'I'd rather not.'

'It's much fatter than my dad's. Why doesn't he use the toilet?'

'Maddie's in the bath again. She'll kill him.' We ran to the bathroom door, giggling, to report him.

F does the talking for me.

'It's you,' he says.

'It's me,' I agree.

'I know why you're here.'

'You do?'

'She wants me out of here,' he says. 'Your Auntie Vagina said as much last time I bumped into her on the stairs.' A quick glance at his face sends me into my room to switch the record off. He follows me in, realizes his mistake – he's not allowed in here – and stands, embarrassed. 'Don't worry about me,' he says. His desperation never fails to bring out the sadist in me.

'When can you move?' As I went towards my bedroom door, he took the hint and backed away. While I locked up, I could feel him too close behind me. 'She doesn't mind paying the removal van. It could be sent at the end of the week.'

'That won't be necessary,' he said, slurring. 'I have nothing to move.'

'Except yourself.'

'Do you want a cup of tea?'

'I don't drink tea.'

'Neither do I.' We forced a laugh.

'I have to go.' I was frightened he might try to touch me. Just as I was about to escape out the front door, he shouted, 'I could always kill myself. Nobody gives a fuck about me anyway. I'll slash my fucking wrists!'

I slammed the door and stood on the landing. The trapdoor leading to the roof caught my eye as I waited for my heart to stop beating hard.

'Maria,' a voice whispers. 'Is that you?'

Down on the next landing, Vagina is peering round her door. 'I didn't see your car outside.'

'I came in a cab.'

'Come in and have a cup of tea.'

'I don't drink tea.'

'I swear I'll use a new tea bag. Honest engine. You can watch me put it in the cup if you like. Or you can have Irn Bru.'

'I'm going back to the hospital to tell her.'

'I'll call you a taxi.'

'I'm going to walk back.'

'Come in for a minute anyway, you're white as a ghost.'

Fat Spam was draped across the sofa – a large, soft Raspberry Knoll with matching armchairs. I understand why Vagina wants Dangerous to buy her a new one.

'Hi,' Spam said, crinkling up her eyes. A copy of *Bride* magazine on her lap. 'I heard you married a millionaire.'

'Millionaires are as poor as everybody else these days.'

'Where did you meet him?'

'In an elevator.' I knew that Dangerous Donald would make a good hero as soon as he walked into the lift. His ambiguous blue-green eyes and cut-glass cheekbones looked great even in the unflattering hospital lighting.

'Trust you,' Fat Spam said, keeping one eye glued to the telly where wee Lulu is singing her latest. 'You know, that could have been me. We went to school together you know.'

'I know.'

'Red hair could be the making of you yet,' Vagina said, bustling in with a tray. Two cups of sweet pale tea for them and a large glass of flat Irn Bru for me. 'I stirred in a spoonful of sugar the way you like it,' she said on cue.

'Thanks.' I forced down a gulp.

'Families,' Vagina said. 'We may hate each other's guts but underneath we share the same flesh and blood.'

'Well,' I said, 'some have more flesh than others.'

'You cheeky wee devil,' she said, throwing a lumpy cushion at me. 'Remember when you were wee you came to stay with us? That time your mummy went mental. It seems like yesterday.' We sat together watching Lulu. She always cheers me up when I see her in the video shop. Silences make Auntie Vagina uncomfortable, even when there's background music. 'You know,' she said to me in a loud whisper, 'that daughter of mine may not be a glamour girl but at least she's never done herself in. Do you want to stay for your tea?'

'What are you having?'

'Steak and chips. I'll use my visitors' pan,' she offered. All the sisters (even Junkie Jenny, who's never up to cooking) have visitors' frying pans reserved for special occasions. It's an offer that's impossible to refuse.

Vertigo

Movies that use real people for their crowd scenes – rather than paid extras – always look fake. The Central Casting rent-a-gang of bored faces is utterly convincing even when you recognize most of them. But is there a fake sky out there that's as good as the real sky?

The sky can never lie, only change its mind. The sky John jumped out of is a thick *Traviata*-blue cluttered with sharp black stars, not the drab sky that's usually above Old Money's building, or the slate sky I'm walking under today. John's sky can only be filmed in my imagination. It's too real to be recreated in real life.

I love this city! The other actors are shorter than me and there's that threat of spiritual thunder. Glasgow has the look of New York and Berlin and has also recently acquired the Japanese tourists.

On my way to the hospital this afternoon, I went into the CCA to hide for a few minutes and browse at the film books. As I was admiring a black-and-white still of Stanley Kubrick's second wife a hand tapped me on the back.

'I was hoping you'd be here,' Lolita said. 'How's your mum?' I can't believe how tiny she is! Every time I see her she's at least a year older. She lives the life I did a decade ago in a flat near Bond Street with a sloping floor and no carpets, staying out all night getting dehydrated. Time rots that brand of glamour. You outgrow it or it drags you down to self-parody.

'Heart still pounding,' I said. 'How did you know?'

'Glasgow grapevine. Have you seen the show yet?'

'The show?' A show for me is a big production number – Judy Garland in *Meet Me in St. Louis*, sneaky Gene Kelly *Singin' in the Rain*, or something with Fred and Ginger.

We wandered along the white corridor to the exhibition space at the back.

'Suicide Notes' has already made a successful tour of America. Death, as Al Alvarez says, is a kind of pornography. Suicide is for the death specialist. You fantasize about doing it so much – it annoys you when somebody else does it first! You're not only jealous, but angry. *How dare you leave me here all alone!* Suicide also provokes a Schadenfreudic smugness. *Huh, couldn't stick it out could you? My life's much worse than yours – and I'm still here!*

Suicide is one of the few things that real life does better than the movies. The letters in this exhibition, even though they're not fascinating, make it possible to eavesdrop on death. In a movie, they'd be a casual aside. But in the true fiction of life, they're real. The success of the suicide is what's important to the voyeur who's seen everything but God's face. Who'd want this boring mail if it had been written in the tears of a failed suicide?

The most popular method of these suicidees is the shot through the skull. Their notes whinge about their white-trash American nightmare. Living alone without insurance in the land where Clark Gable was invented, it's tough having too many dreams that never come true.

'John didn't leave a note, did he?' Lolita asked, hoping to catch me out.

'He was a man of action.'

'I loved him, too,' she said, flicking her unnaturally blonde hair back. Particles of L'Oreal Gold (firm hold) hairspray clung to its shafts. 'I see you're still wearing your locket.' His heart arrived in the mail after he died. He had posted it to me on time for the six-thirty collection and jumped at seven – our favourite number for mystical reasons and because life begins at seven. From your first birthday until your sixth, time is eternal. Suddenly everything speeds up and you're twenty. Thirty. Pretending not to dread forty. Some days you remember everything.

'I have to go to the hospital,' I said.

'I'll come with you.'

'Maddie can't stand you.'

'So?'

In the daylight, she said, 'You look tired. What age are you these days?'

'I stopped lying about my age when I was twenty-five.'

'I'm still at it,' she admitted. 'Don't you think you act the age you're supposed to be?'

'Is that a good thing?'

'It keeps you young.'

'Why do you want to stay young?'

'Everybody does.'

'Do they?' We both bought a frozen yogurt lolly from a stand and walked along sucking them. A dirty child passed us in High Street, staring at my Strawberry Daiquiri on a stick. I could give him the money for one but it would set a bad example. He has self-mutilation written all over his future face. He might grow up to be a gigolo – expecting rewards from smiling strangers.

'What are you thinking about?' she asked like a jealous boyfriend.

'Clark Gable's moustache.'

'Do you think he was gay?'

'I couldn't care less.'

'I snogged a man with a moustache last week.'

'I don't want the sordid details.'

'Who said it was sordid? He's really minted.'

I finished my lolly first. She said, 'I'm amazed at us meeting up here when we both live in London!' I'm not. Lolita is famous for her Glasgow junkets. She can't keep away from the place.

'Look what the cat dragged in,' said Maddie, audacious in her sugar-pink satin fur-trimmed Frederick's of Hollywood nightie. The sort of tack glamour that needs irony and an audience.

'Very Dianne Brill,' Lolita said. 'Can I try on your shoes?' She kicked off her red plastic Patrick Cox sandals, slipping her petite feet into Maddie's Manolo mules.

'They're like big boats on me,' Lolita said clacking around in them.

'I have important decisions to discuss with my daughter,' Maddie said. Now that F's got his marching orders, it's crucial to choose between the crimson velvet furnishings and the *Traviata*-blue. Perhaps both – but not in the same room! At all costs, we need to avoid the crucifixion look.

'I only came in to say hello,' Lo said.

'Nothing better to do with yourself as usual,' Maddie snapped back.

I walked my ex-best friend back to the lift. 'Let's go to a movie later,' she said, as we waited. 'Do you know what's on?' she asked, puckering her brow. She looks a bit like Theresa Russell in *Bad Timing* when she does that. Just a little.

'No,' I lied. I listened to the recorded messages of the Salon, Odeon, Grosvenor and MGM cinemas last night when I couldn't sleep. I know their programmes by heart, but I couldn't sit in the dark with her! Anyway, she's a victim film fanatic. Anything with a wounded woman appeals to her. *Dance with a Stranger. The Purple Rose of Cairo.* Smack me in the jaw, I need masochism! Still, there's a great bit in *Dance* when Ruth asks (her spare boyfriend) Desmond, 'Like a banana?' When he refuses, she says casually, 'I don't blame you. They're terrible things.' Freudian or what. 'I'll call you.'

'I'm staying with the parents.' Where else? She can't afford a hotel. I watched her until the lift doors closed. Who would have thought it? She's nothing to me now, but all day I'm going to worry. Before going to bed, when she's been up all night raging, does she swallow vitamin C? Does she use extra strong condoms? Is she saving up for a facelift?

Because she's a part of my past, I don't want to witness her decay. Over and over these signs appear, warning me: *Dead, John is safe.* He's up in H doing the tango with Anna Kavan — or maybe discussing syringes. Or having a martini with Scott Fitzgerald, analysing the seductive thrills of self-destruction. Who knows what would have happened if he'd gone on living.

'Scour those shoes of mine with TCP, will you?' Maddie ordered when I went back to her bedside. 'The idea of it! You had a hundred pair of shoes when you were wee – and your feet were still growing. You've never put on someone else's shoes in your life!'

I picked a piece of cotton wool out of her blue crystal storage jar and smothered it with TCP, giving the inside of her shoe a quick wipe.

'That one would make the perfect girlfriend for Charlie Manson.'

'What are you talking about?'

'Well she's wee and weird isn't she? And so was he.'

'Friend of yours?'

'You know fine and well he's been on the telly millions of times.' Lolita is the type who'd write love letters to lifers. 'I don't know what your brother ever saw in her.' Maddie sighed. 'You were always better looking but of course there's no comparison between the two of you now. She looks even older than me!'

'She's not that bad,' I said, tossing the cotton wool in the bin and running my fingers under the hot tap.

'I'm no Princess Diana,' Maddie said, 'but that friend of yours is a total mess.'

'What's Diana got to do with it?'

'Well,' Maddie checked her face in the magnifying side of her compact as she spoke, 'she has the money to spend on herself.' Denying her wealth is Maddie's prime obsession. No matter how poor you are – there's always somebody richer. Boom, boom.

'A lot of rich people are dogs.'

'At least they can afford it.'

Huh? I should have smelled a rat. Even for Maddie, this was a weird dialogue. She must be on drugs. She hadn't even mentioned how much weight Lolita had put on! As soon as we finished discussing the statistical likelihood of being fat and poor, or rich and thin, the cunt tried to extract another pound of flab from me.

The Hound of the Baskervilles

Sherlock Holmes always gets a full moon. Full moons make me impulsive but Basil Rathbone's in control when he's under the big white artificial moon in Studio B. His elongated face suits the wooden interiors of those Holmes mystery movies.

Of course, it isn't just the full moon. For sentimental reasons, I always act weird in the run up to the crucifixion. But tonight's insomnia is her fault. I can't believe I've allowed her to annoy me. Though now I have an excuse to go back to London. My doctor will give me something for the rest of Lent. Dr Grant understands the danger of too many nightmares. Too bad I didn't have time to see him before rushing up here.

The message light on the phone's flashing. She's been calling for hours. If I didn't enjoy hearing it ring I would unplug it. The unanswered sound reminds me of *Once Upon A Time in America* when Bob De Niro (who used to be glam but isn't any more) is calling his dead girlfriend, Eve.

'Let me explain,' she called after me as I stormed out of the hospital. Characters in movies are always explaining. Cary Grant explains to Joan Fontaine in *Suspicion*. She half-believes he isn't going to kill her. Cary refuses to listen to Ingrid Bergman's explanations in *Notorious*. Jimmy Stewart perversely doesn't give

Kim Novak a chance to explain in *Vertigo*. Explaining means making excuses for inexcusable behaviour. Excuses have only temporary uses.

Sherlock Holmes is on a moor, one of his favourite haunts, and I'm in Maddie's bed in Devonshire Gardens watching him. I've seen *The Hound of the Baskervilles* a million times – it's the sort of movie she allowed us to stay up late for – but I can't follow it. Not because it's complicated but because of its imaginative simplicity. Since it's obvious that the goodies will temporarily triumph over the baddies, there's no need to pay tense attention. The pictures are allowed to provoke your own daydreams of good and evil with you as the hero.

Even though I've emptied the contents of her mini-bar into my mouth, I'm still going to be awake at The End. I haven't stayed up all night watching TV since my illness. The drugs that were killing the germs in my tubercular toe used to keep me awake. It was great, lying in bed with the latest rental from Prime Time, knowing there was nothing to wake up for the next day except the afternoon movie. Shock protected me in those days.

Maddie didn't visit me when I was sick. Of course, the last person I want to see when I'm not well is a doctor; and the second-last person is my mother. She wrote to me saying, 'Nobody catches a contagious disease unless they're up to no good,' enclosing a cheque to see me through my convalescence.

The mattress on this four-poster's still rancid with her perfume even though the linen's been changed. Its brocade curtains are distracting my attention from the screen, but they can't move me to another room 'without Mrs Money's permission'.

'This suite is wildly popular with young business types,' the room service waiter told me when he brought the tray of Black Russians, eyes peeled for the party. Giving him a pound, I slammed the door in his ungrateful face. Tipping is tiring. They expect at least £5 for every delivery because Maddie's renting the most expensive rooms in the place.

Trying to act casual, the cunt asked, 'When did you say your father was moving?' She'd been unplugged from the scan and her disconnected drip was on a dusty shelf in the corner. She exposed her teeth too quick for me to be certain her right fang was smeared with Honey Honey lipstick. If she's back on the make-up, she's up to something.

'I told you. He'll be out by the end of the week. His brother's taking him.'

'He needn't bother,' she said. 'I have a feeling I'm better off in the sun.' Adding insult to injury, she picked up the *Vogue Casa* I'd been ordered to fetch. 'There's nothing in here I fancy anyway as a colour scheme. You can drop by tomorrow and tell him he can stay on. I'm out of here as soon as Mr Blur gives me the OK. It's dead boring, Glasgow.'

'You bought your lobotomy in the wrong shop if you think I'm going back to see him again. Tell him yourself.'

'That's the thanks I get,' she said. 'I did everything for you and you're full of ingratitude. Oh well, maybe your Auntie Vagina will have a wee word with him. You know she used to fancy your dad?'

'Don't change the subject.'

'What subject?' She touched her heart with her painted fingernails.

'Has Jonathan been in touch by any chance?'

'Jonathan who?'

'Jonathan the American. You know, the dead glam man you met on the steps of Pizza Hut – even though you could both afford lobster. That wee millionaire you went to New Mexico with because he's a sun lover and you're an artist although you definitely don't share a house together shsh don't say Double Bed.'

'Oh, that Jonathan. As a matter of fact I'm thinking of taking a cruise. Remember *The Oriana?*'

'I'm not senile.' We sailed to New York on *The Oriana* when I was wee. Maddie was furious because Cary Grant and Dyan Cannon were supposed to be on board but they had crossed on the trip before us! The whole journey I had to listen to her ranting about how we were going to be raped the minute we arrived in New York. But it was all right in the end, because the shops in Fifth Avenue are the best in the world, and they made a lot of us in the Plaza Hotel.

'Well there's a new *Oriana*, I saw it on the telly. That Cary Grant may fall for me yet.'

'Cary Grant is dead.'

'Same difference. Stupid name for a man anyway.' Archie Leach concealed his round shoulders behind Savile Row tailoring and became Cary Grant with a little help from a suntan and an empty soul.

The Baskerville hound howls and The End comes up on the screen. That doesn't always happen these days when a movie's over. Those two words are exciting and addictive, like the seductive kiss signifying an X Certificate.

I scanned the hotel's video library list for possibilities. Of course, I've seen them all before. That makes disappointment impossible. John's favourite movie, *The Picture of Dorian Gray*, stands out. Thank God for the all night cocktail menu. Being awake at dawn used to make me feel guilty but I've taken my hero's advice and given up guilt for Lent.

If the sleep train doesn't come in five minutes flat I'll order

111

a Kir Royale and a Long Island Iced Tea, and not tip at all this time!

Lolita will be asleep on the sixties sofa in her parents' council flat. I still know her family's number by heart. The phone rings and rings, waking no one. She's out dancing! The idea horrifies me. We always dreaded growing up to be old swingers. I remember her on the dancefloor, saying, 'Those tarts are at least twenty-four,' disgusted by two girls in truly shocking pink sequined boob tubes who were aware of being stared at for the wrong reasons.

We were out every night except a Monday when nothing happened. It was impossible waking up for school. I used to go in at eleven, missing calculus, private study and playtime. Mr Sherlock the Headmaster sent for Maddie.

'She misses maths class every morning,' he said. Maddie gave him the silent treatment. 'It's an important subject,' he said, apology lurking behind his glasses.

'Have you seen her report card?' Maddie asked, pulling it out of her bag. 'She gets 100 per cent for maths every time. What's your problem?'

'100 per cent,' he repeated. 'Do you cheat?'

'Not as far as I know.' At school, I was the master of the ambiguous reply.

'The cheek of it!' Maddie said. 'She's never cheated in her life. She has a perfect memory – inherited it from me.'

'Well,' Mr Sherlock said, alarmed, 'the law still requires her to start school at nine.'

'She likes her beauty sleep,' Maddie told him, putting her suede gloves back on. 'Girls will be girls.'

Tonight, I'd just like to sleep. The birds are singing. That's what's wrong with this hotel! There's no pollution outside.

Even though it's almost in the city centre, the view from the window is twee green.

But I love hotels – especially when I'm not paying for them. I love shoes. I could try on her pink patent stilettos and stick them back under the bed without disinfecting them! I love perfume. I could go and take a bath and pour in a whole bottle of her Chanel.

Most of all, I'm terrified. I don't want to die. Insomnia always reminds me. But I don't want to live for ever! I have to escape, and now I have a really good excuse to leave her in the lurch. She's behaved badly. I don't have to stay here. And when she's out of hospital, I don't have to go on a tourist bus round what's left of Hollywood with her. I don't have to do anything. Because even though my mother, the only mother I have, now has a bad heart and is probably going to die soon; I'm going to die too. Every second death is closer and closer. YIKES!

Necropolis

Stealing the advantage, I hid my bag in Sister's cupboard and waited until Maddie had confessed her own travel plans before telling her.

'Something's come up,' I said, acting casual. 'I have to go back to London today.'

'You mean you're sulking.'

'We're selling our place. I have to help my husband.'

'I never heard of anything like it in my life! I've sold millions of flats – entire buildings sometimes – and I've never had the falderal you seem to have. What do you think lawyers are for?'

'We're not made of money like you. We have to get rid of it before the roof caves in.' Dangerous bought the Georgian mansion on the Northumberland coast soon after we met in the elevator and married. The sea cured my consumption, but at heart we're city people.

'I have to work tomorrow anyway. I'll miss my flight if I don't go now.' Streaky mascara tears were threatening behind her made-up eyes.

'Jon wanted to meet you.'

'We can meet some other time.'

'You'll never come and visit me. Couldn't you at least wait until I'm released from here? I'll never see you again.'

'You could visit me,' I said rashly.

'We could, couldn't we? After all, there's no reason why we have to fly back from here. Remember that time we stayed at The Ritz when you were wee?'

'The manager asked us to leave.'

'Only because of your roller skating! He'd be delighted to see us.'

'I doubt if he's still alive.'

'Look up the number for me.'

'Look it up yourself, I have to go.'

'Thanks for the sympathy. Remember you were in here when you were wee – having your wee tonsils taken out?'

'I'm going.'

'Aren't you going to kiss your mother?' John always squirmed when she tried to touch him. He preferred being slapped to being pawed. I allowed her to molest my cheek.

'You know, I was always dead jealous of you and him. The way you stuck together. He turned you against me.'

'I have to go.'

Outside, letting empty cabs fly past, I detoured into the cathedral.

There was nobody about. It's great being in a building with a high roof. It reminds you that God's always up there, watching. But I couldn't talk to Him in there – it's the wrong faith.

Any minute now someone could walk in and see me progressing through the narrow temple towards the altar, seven stolen postcards in my right hand, eyes trained on the stained-glass ceiling. I dumped my bag in a pew, stopped to light a candle, then found the secret room.

*   *   *

'This place is great,' John said, 'like being in a movie.'

I could feel his breath on my neck as we sprawled on the dark stone slabs, bare summer legs numb.

'She'll kill us,' I said, keen to soil my starched white cotton dress.

'She can try,' he said. We must have been really young. He was acting like the leader. My legs were skeletal.

The room isn't pitch black like the ebony hole of hopefulness in my memory. It's dim, like blindness, and the way I imagine Joan Collins's bathroom – so that if she gets up in the middle of the night her wigless reflection will be less frightening.

My patent leather shoes, polished this morning by the valet, stick out like cat's eyes at the end of my DKNY legs. During the day I'm too self-conscious to talk to God. Being in a church reminds me of my spiritual vertigo. At night, with a view of the stars, I can practise acting casual before asking God for a favour. I need to talk to Him soon. But not here, not today. I have to go or I'll miss my flight.

Outside, I can see the Necropolis across the road but there isn't time to climb the hill and stand beside Old Money's grave staring over the city. Of course, I could lose my discount, take the next flight. I'm made of Money! That was her joke. Ha fucking Ha.

The Necropolis makes me think of that bit in *Gone With the Wind* when Scarlett O'Hara eats the earth. The cool wind is like clean skin and Stolichnaya. If John was buried here?

I should never have allowed them to burn him. When he visited me in New York he promised, 'If you die first I'll steal your body from the funeral parlour.'

'Why?' It was his last night. We were in the cinema on 8th

116

Street. As we were buying our tickets for *New York, New York*, Debbie Harry walked in wearing a headscarf over her dark roots. We couldn't keep our eyes off her.

'Why what?' he asked when we were seated in the front row licking ice lollies.

'Why would you steal my corpse?'

'So she can't stick you in the ground with Old Money,' John said.

'She'll die before us then we'll get her money.'

'Not a chance,' he said.

'What will you do with my body?'

'Have it preserved then book into a lot of different hotels and keep you in the wardrobe.'

'It's a toss up between that and the worms in the Necropolis,' I said.

If John was buried I'd wish he'd been burned.

When we picked and paid for his cheap pine coffin from Bob Price the Funeral Director I had an instant vision of it sliding down to the furnace room and felt as if I was in an elevator that had lost its brakes. Always crashing in a different car, with no bones left to cling on to. Obliteration always appealed to John. He wanted a Viking's funeral, like Gary Cooper in *Beau Geste*. I cry laughing every time I see that movie about three brothers who don't quite go the gay way, not to mention the elusive but memorable Burden the butler.

I'd hate John to still be alive. Dead, he means everything. In real life I could have stopped loving him years ago.

Decisively, I stopped a taxi. Catching sight of my face in the rearview, I'm relieved to see it looks great.

'Going on your holidays?' the driver asked me.

'Going to the movies,' I muttered.

'At the airport?' he persisted. Taxi drivers never take the hint. They're so narcissistic – if they want to talk, you've had it.

'They show a film on the plane.'

That's what's wrong with me! I haven't been to the movies for days. I'll get a new *Time Out* and scan the listings. Dangerous isn't expecting me today. As soon as I reach London I'll head for one of my cinemas.

Hollywood, Heaven, Hell

'There's no substitute for what you really want.'
Rudolph Valentino

Dead Cinema

Tuesday night is murder night. I'm on my way to the Fun Film Club in Wormwood Scrubs to show a video of *Reservoir Dogs* to my homicidal rapists, baba bashers, and lazy wife killers. *Reservoir Dogs* is more popular than *Pulp Fiction*, though that has its fans.

'You can identify with *Dogs*,' Johnnie the drug killer explains. 'It's dead romantic.' Tarantino's uplifting movies are guaranteed to cheer up anyone with a sense of humour.

'Going to visit your boyfriend?' the nosy cab driver asks as we speed along Ladbroke Grove towards the prison gates, already over-familiar from Ealing comedies.

'I'm going to work.' As Maddie says, this is a job for a queer hawk. Sleaze intrigued me as a teenager, but now that I'm older and more idealistic crims bore me. Their glamour is a decoy. It's easy to forget this – because most people don't know too many real murderers. And there's a lineage of charming, sensitive, superbrain psychos immortalized in celluloid: Mr Blond, Travis Bickle, Dr Lecter, Alex in *Clockwork Orange*.

'We've picked the wrong night for it,' the cabbie says.

'Huh?'

'Work.' The weather's gone bananas. Outside, people are drinking wine on street corners. 'Let's hope it keeps up for the

121

weekend.' Let's hope it doesn't. I have a busy day tomorrow. Doctor, hair, facial. You're not supposed to have a facial the same day as a life-changing trip to the hairdresser's! I'm breaking the rules, asking for disaster, but Dr Grant will sort me out. He isn't a man to argue with a tragic anniversary. Doctors divide into two: the ones who give you what you want, and the ones who're hell-bent on stopping you having it.

The cab drops me at the arched gate. Waving my pass at the grumpy guard, I go through the sliding steel doors and collect my heavy keyring of big Alice in Wonderland keys. Only one key opens the barbed-wire gates in the compound, the others are included for the larger than life effect.

Going towards the small room adjoining the toilet where the Fun Film Club takes place, I stick close to the edges in case there's any flying ka-ka tonight. Half of the murderers don't have toilets in their cells yet. Which would you prefer? Throwing a shit bomb at someone from outside; or sleeping with it under the bed until slop out?

The dogs, sniffing for heroin, remind me of East Berlin before it was ruined. Where were you the night in November 1989 when the six o'clock news announced that The Wall was coming down? I was in my flat without furniture, sobbing, 'They're ruining Berlin.' The ultimate noir city, with its authentic bullet-smattered walls, is the only place I could have committed suicide. Now it doesn't exist, I have another excuse to go on living!

When I first came to work here it seemed like a laugh. Reality and fantasy were separate in my mind but not my imagination. I was in the dark about mundane murder.

Murder is in the present tense. At least, it is in the movies.

122

The camera focuses on excitement, fear, regret. That tragic irreparable moment. In real life, you can rent another video. Actually being murdered wouldn't be nearly as much fun as watching it in a movie, though I'm not volunteering to test my theory.

My murderers are smoking in the screening room. No hot-dogs, but a variety of rustling sweeties.

'Oh-O, Miss Whiplash is in a bad mood again,' Scratcher says.

'Go fuck yourself with a banana, Fuckwit,' I reply, putting the cassette in the machine, adjusting the tracking. I'm allowed to swear because I'm their idea of a middle-class woman.

'Does that mean you haven't brought me an Easter egg?' Scratcher persists.

'I'll give you a hammer and nails if you promise to crucify yourself.' Everybody laughs. I switch out the fluorescent light, the cue for silence. You have to watch movies in the dark. Darkness is dangerous. It camouflages the flaws in the audience as well as highlighting the screen. Maddie has offered (even though she doesn't have any money) to pay me not to come here any more. 'Something terrible could happen to you,' she says, in her ghoulish maternal voice. But I have my bodyguard, Johnnie, a teenage weightlifter.

I'm sitting between Christopher and Victor. Johnnie's behind me. Usually I sit with my back to the door, but I trust Johnnie. Young and serene, he's playing the part of the charming, clever, courageous murderer still lingering in my imagination. He's a fantasy enabler, but he'll outgrow it. In a couple of years youth will have frozen into something more painful.

Everybody smells. I stink of Chanel taken from Maddie's hotel room. Johnnie has recently showered. He uses coal tar soap to quell the scent of D-Wing. Vick has been eating cabbage.

123

Chris is drunk again. Scratcher is wearing his delouse powder. It exacerbates the itching. Other smells crowd into the edges of the small room as the cool *Dogs* gang discuss the ethics of tipping. I keep looking at the bolted window.

We're a restless audience. Fast-forwarding, rewinding, watching our backs. None of my murderers have tried to escape the way murderers in crime thrillers always do. For my murderers, a life sentence sometimes isn't a deterrent but an incentive. An opportunity never to have to make a decision while secretly indulging omnipotent re-runs of that squalid moment of power: that murder.

Andy with the furrowed forehead in the front row committed the understandable *crime passionel* after catching his wife shagging a nigger under the duvet his grandmother gave them as a wedding present. Ten out of ten for motive, Andy, any man would have been mad. But why did you chop the slut up, wrap her in binliners, and distribute her unevenly into other people's garbage pails? Never heard of divorce, mate? Andy scowls at the boiling kettle by his elbow. 'He will be all right,' his psychiatric report reassures, 'so long as he doesn't snap.' Snap what?

Next to him, crouching on the floor, is a brown man who strangled his wife because they were 'in England'. *Hey, wife doesn't look good in this light. Can't afford a return plane ticket. A-ha – I'll strangle the bitch.* This creature doesn't look as if he has the energy to strangle anyone. His wife must have been quite a specimen – one of those victims you see all the time on late-night TV being pursued by stalkers, and you have to sit there shouting, 'Buy yourself a hammer you idiot and knock him over the head with it!'

The brown geezer feels me looking at him. His head turns anti-clockwise, thinks better of it, and sinks back forward. I can just picture him sitting with his psychiatrist, struggling to come up with a convincing excuse. And what's the message in his story? Don't emigrate with your husband – at least, not to England.

Vick offered me a crisp. 'I didn't know anyone still ate smoky bacon,' I say, taking a handful. Vick goes red. He needs to be liked. When I make eye contact with him, he looks away, wondering if I know. 'He has bad eyes,' Maddie used to say about John. She tried her best, but couldn't like him. And me, I love him like it was yesterday, I love him like I love all the dead cinemas in the world – regretting they're gone, even if I neglected them when alive.

On my right, Chris snorts, fidgets, unties his shoelace. He's not sure about this movie even though he's seen it before. Blood disturbs him. He stabbed a girl he'd never seen before in his puff thirty-one times in the stomach and chest. 'I did it on impulse,' he told his psychiatrist. 'She shouldn't have moved into the room next door.'

The smell is upsetting me. I can't bear it. Obsessively checking my watch, waiting for the bell. I'm not coming back. Why struggle on until the last screening advertised on the Fun Film Club poster? They won't like *Mean Streets* anyway. Too moody and subtle; too sad to see Bobby De Niro before he went mediocre. What's the point in stiffupperlipping along? There's something irritating about leaving a movie before the end, even when you've lost interest in the plot.

How far can lice jump? Scratcher, whose name isn't changed to protect the guilty but because I can't remember it, is sitting as far away from me as is possible in a cupboard. But I'm aware of his index fingernail, the same one he uses to pick his nose, hacking off his skin. Sawing his neck, turning it red, though not the vivid red John achieved with a sparkly razor on his inner arm – that old teenage fetish. Lolita and I watched but didn't join in.

'He's dead brave,' she said.

'He's a fucking idiot,' I said, admiring him anyway.

Chris doesn't want a crisp. He pushes Vick's packet away and says to me, 'You're sick. These fucking movies you like are fucking sick.' Johnnie stares him out. We share a seductive smile. I'm dreaming about my shower at home in my clean white flat.

Vick offers me a sip of his Ribena. He isn't surprised when I decline to share the straw. Vick battered a baby to death. It wasn't his baby. Just some baby his girlfriend was baby-sitting. Vick was unemployed and this baby was getting on his nerves the way it was just lying there doing fuck all. It took about twenty minutes to murder it, he guesses, because his girlfriend was watching *EastEnders* and it had been on for a bit before he started beating the baba's brains out. Vick is 'sorry'. It says so in his file. Hey that's great, Vick. Maybe you should write to the parents? *Sorry, your baby was just in the right place at the wrong time. Nobody's fault. Sorry.*

Chris can't stand it any longer. While Mr Blond does his groovy dance, Chris stands up and bangs his head against the cupboard wall, keeping the beat with Stealer's Wheel. The others stamp their feet, chanting, 'Shut the fuck up, Shut the fuck up.' Everybody joins in except black Bill, who's kept a low profile since I pigged him for complaining about *Performance*. 'That was on telly years ago,' black Bill said. And I went for him. I enjoy my work, putting the frighteners on tawdry little twerps.

Scratcher turns the sound up. Chris wails louder, giving us an excuse to rewind the tape and watch Mr Blond carve off the policeman's ear again.

Sounding calm, I say, 'If you don't like the film go bugger somebody in the toilets.'

'Sick bitch,' he says. Chris is the perfect foil for the censorship contingent. He invited me to move into his cell with him 'on a trial basis' – even though we haven't watched a single film about experimental relationships. An impressionable idiot doesn't need to get his daft ideas from a movie. The lines between art and reality are blurred for many people. They don't all choose the psycho role. Admittedly, anyone who doesn't know that kicking a baby's head in is evil is unlikely to be cured watching *Reservoir Dogs*. But censoring art to make it comfortable to the mediocracy will not prevent crimes of boredom either.

Johnnie is twisting Chris's arm behind his back.

'I was joking!' big Chris says to me. 'But why can't we have *The Flintstones* or *Superman* or something for a change?'

'Shut up, Fuckwit,' Johnnie says. Johnnie's always considering my welfare. Last week he gave me a lovely knife with a mother-of-pearl handle, explaining how to stab someone in the kidney. 'The last thing you want to do,' he told me, face white with concern, 'is to allow him to get his hands on your weapon.'

'Who?'

'Whoever. You have to disable him.'

'Thanks.'

I left the screening room and went along the corridor to talk to Gerry the Cat. After all, I've seen the movie millions of times. I know what happens. Tonight I'm not in the mood for a happy ending.

Gerry the Cat is sitting behind the guard's desk, guarding. He has his walkie-talkie, his book, his can of Diet Pepsi. I know I'm sailing downstream in a banana boat with no break when I can't make up my mind which can of Pepsi to buy and which one to leave in the shop. They all look the same. Seeing his can reminds me that I was too indecisive earlier on to pick one of my own.

'Ah-hu,' he says instead of hello.

'What're you reading?' He upturns his book. *The Beautiful and Damned*. OK.

'What's the movie tonight?'

'*Reservoir Dogs* again.'

'I'll have to see that sometime.' He's dying to get back to his book. No one ever talks to him. My chat makes him uneasy.

'Why are you called Gerry the Cat?'

'I told you. It has something to do with *Tom and Jerry*.'

'The cartoon, right?'

'Yeah.'

'Jerry's the mouse.'

'Say no more,' he says. I don't. I go back and watch the rest of the movie, thinking about Anthony Patch and Gloria Gilbert, rich residents of New York, New York. *Anthony Patch and Gloria Gilbert are very beautiful*. It says so on the cover of Gerry the Cat's book.

Outside, my cab's waiting.

'In for a visit?' the driver asks, hurtling towards Ladbroke Grove.

At this time of night, Fuckwit? But I know my lines. I've done this scene before. 'I work there.'

'Mmm,' he leers. 'What do you do?'

'Show movies.'

'You mean if I get banged up we can go to the movies together?'

'You'd have to do a murder.'

'Why's that?'

'It's only murderers that are allowed to join the Fun Film Club.'

'Perverse,' he says, cackling. There's a beautiful silence. Then he asks, 'What kind of murder?'

'Take your pick. They're all the same.' The heart stops. The cause of death is variable but the same: the heart always stops beating without God's permission.

An item comes over the radio about slanty-eyed parents selling their two-year-olds into prostitution. I can only half hear – the cabbie is still trying to keep the murder conversation going – and I only half want to hear. I can't fucking bear it. I wish they would murder their children. Why doesn't God do something! I feel pompous and angry, wondering if praying really hard will help? The movies constantly reveal that anything's usually possible.

When my building appears up ahead, comforting and white, I start forgetting the wee prossies and wondering what's on TV.

Dangerous is sitting on our pale perfect carpet watching *Jagged Edge*.

'Hurry up,' he says, 'it's just started.' Even though I know already that Jeff Bridges is the ice-man killer, I always want it not to be him when his mask is removed at the end. His guilt makes the movie memorable.

At the adverts, Dangerous brings a glass of chilled chablis into the bathroom for me.

'Hello, Lady Macbeth. Your mother's on the phone,' he shouts, above the noise of the shower.

'What does she want?'

'To talk to you!'

'Tell her I'll call her tomorrow.' His footsteps disappear back to *Jagged Edge*. If a lifetime as a movie junkie has taught me anything, it's that catastrophe is usually followed by resurrection.

The phone rang as soon as I was dried and sitting sipping my chablis, watching the bit when Jeff first kisses Glenn Close – nobody's favourite sexpot.

'Yes?'

'Just wanted to make sure you weren't murdered in that queer hawk job of yours.'

'I'm still alive.'

'Good. You haven't forgotten about Thursday?'

'Thursday . . .'

'Cheeky devil – be at my hotel at eleven sharp. It would be too much to expect you to meet me at the airport.' That means, don't meet me – I'll be with the famous Jonathan. 'Does Dangerous know about dinner on Friday?'

'The double date? Oh no, I forgot to ask him. He's probably going to be at Mass all day Friday too.'

'What! All day? Surely he can't be planning to spend the whole of Good Friday on his knees – Catholic or no Catholic.'

'He's not sure if he can have dinner with a married woman and her boyfriend, not on a religious holiday.'

'Jon is not my boyfriend! He's a very nice man.'

'See you on Thursday. Wait a minute – where are you staying again?'

'The Ritz! 150 Piccadilly at Arlington Street. You can't miss it. Take a taxi if you can't find it.'

Marnie

On Wednesday morning her voice came on cue over the machine as I was rushing out to see my doctor.

'Are you there?' she asked. 'I know you. You're probably on a plane to Tokyo right now. Anything to avoid me.' Her old voice is pleading with me to pick up the phone, put her out of her misery. But if I'm late for Dr Grant, I'll be late for Darren and then Janet. Hair and skin are important. And after my hair colour and facial, I have a million other things to do – like queue for my prescription, my insurance for the Easter weekend. Maybe I'll even have my nails done, to please Maddie, even though it gives me brain-damage sitting, intoxicated by the pong, waiting for the paint to dry.

Short rounded deep-ruby fingernails are one of life's essential inessentials. Like Chinese yellow walls in a candlelit dining room. *Traviata*-blue satin pillowslips under the head of a sleeping angel. Enormous clean soft white towels like that set hanging in my bathroom.

In the taxi to Harley Street, I checked my face in my compact. Insomnia sweats impurities out of your skin, giving you an

131

ethereal glow. When I make my entrance, Dr Grant always says, 'You look great.'

Usually when I go to see him it's for sleeping pills. He gives me them to consolidate trust, and because I always ask in the run-up to John's big day – the right time in my psychotic calendar, when it's advisable to grant my wishes.

Most nights I'm in bed catching my sleep train without any chemical help before you can say choo-choo. Saving the pills for special occasions, taking as required rather than desired. It's comforting to know they're waiting under the bed.

Dr Grant knows all my secrets. He looks like Colonel Gadaffi, but doesn't wear the tent dresses. I wouldn't actually seduce him, but sometimes make him imagine it. Improbable fantasies have more power. The superficial intimacy of the doctor–patient relationship is bound to provoke hostility or attraction. Alone, eyes locked, sharing lies. He wants me to be Marnie, and I pretend he's (early period) Sean Connery – at least, for the duration of the consultation.

The atmosphere of forbidden sexuality comes from that intense eye contact, his interest in the stories I tell him, the impossibility of a physical examination. And it's pretty clear that I'm Dr Grant's fantasy patient. This makes me feel better.

'Beautiful, but strange,' he says, smiling, as he writes the prescription for my Temazepam, and the occasional bottle of Codeine – just in case. Withdrawal symptoms from jellies include – incompatibly – insomnia and nightmares; but also the more attractive forgetfulness and weight loss. But I don't need to withdraw, I've got Dr Grant. He understands that a little morphine derivative now and again is better than a one-off big suicidal injection. Or is it?

When Dr Grant explained the statistical relationship between parasuicide and suicide, I was shocked. I'd been sure all those pretend suicide attempts – walking into the road with my eyes shut, swallowing a mouthful of pills then sicking them up – were nothing more than embarrassing insurance. I'd been playing at suicide for so long (and making sure *nobody* knew about it), I wasn't actually going to do it. I'm too scared it won't work. And even more scared that it will!

That's why I envy John. He had many a cowardly bone in his body, but at the final moment he didn't lack courage. I'm scared to die. Even though I know that dying doesn't have to be bad. It isn't the same for everybody. And, really, I want to live. Opposite longings cancel each other out, leaving their victim in vulgar compromise.

Of course even though I know that Dr Grant can't help, he does help. It's soothing to believe, if only in his room, that he can make me better. Dangerous – who really knows my secrets – says that I'm frighteningly sane. My terror disturbs him. Seeing him sad makes me worse. I feel deep regret for confessing, like the kind I suffer when I resist a pair of shoes I want to buy then go back later to find them lost forever on someone else's wee feet. If Dangerous doesn't know that I still love John, it isn't real. Of course he does know. But so long as we don't talk about it, it can't kill me. That's where analysts go wrong. Understanding why you're miserable is useless, the trick is stopping misery. Repression, control, buttoning your lip: all underestimated strategies. There are few things that can't be cured with a champagne-tequila or a long sleep in the New York Plaza after seven martinis and a Swedish massage.

The hero of *The Leopard Man* and his *femme fatale* start the movie selfish, and end admiring the strength that comes through courage. That's the ideal – not blabbing your guts over the person you love.

If Dr Grant isn't genuinely interested in my case (and after a longish career of cases, who could fault him for that), his performance is flawless. He has an excuse to watch my every move. And he makes the most of it. He looks sad when I leave him, but not too sad. Because I need him to be strong. I need to imagine him always in that room playing the part of my doctor, waiting for me to come back and be cured again.

I'd hate him to die. Movie stars are better off dead but not doctors. Without Dr Grant or Darren the hairdresser or Janet the skin therapist I'd have blackheads, dark roots, more sleepless nights than I could enjoy. But without my collection of dead glam videos, I wouldn't have a future.

As the taxi stopped outside Dr Grant's building, I glanced up to see if he was at the window.

'Are they watching us?' Elizabeth Taylor asks Montgomery Clift as they close-dance at the party, playing the parts of Angela and George. They're not in the sun, they're under a key light – their beauty illuminated before it's lost. Later, he plays her doctor in *Suddenly, Last Summer* – protecting her from a lobotomy, while in real life she saves him from the sack for forgetting his lines.

My memory gets on my nerves. Dreaming improves the memory. Sleeping pills are supposed to suppress dreaming and encourage memory loss. But I have my daymares just the same, with John's face on the horizon. And I'm so fucking bored with this illogical feeling that most of it's my fault.

Going up in the lift, I could smell my own perfume – a sign of vulgarity, except it's a good smell. And Dr Grant looks like the sort of man who likes a woman to be generous with the Chanel. Ava Gardner and Lana Turner smile like they lavish it on.

His redhead receptionist, who isn't his type, says, 'The doctor is waiting for you, Miss Money.' They always call me that, even though I've admitted to being married. Sometimes, when we're having a little chat, Dr Grant tries to blame Dangerous for my 'strange thoughts'. But that's a male rivalry thing. Before I met Dangerous, I was definitely stranger. Easter affected me even more in the days before I was happy.

Dr Hope was sitting behind Dr Grant's bottle-green leather desk.

'Good Morning, Miss Money,' he said, reading my file. 'I'm Dr Hope.'

'Where's Dr Grant?'

'Dr Grant is away, Miss Money.'

'Away where?'

'Didn't Mrs Crawford inform you?'

'Certainly not!'

'Dr Grant is away until next week. Perhaps you'd prefer to make another appointment?'

'No,' I replied, relieved. 'It's OK. So long as he isn't dead.'

'Well, what can we do for you?'

'I'd like thirty-three Temazepam.'

'Why?'

'Well, it's almost Easter. And Christ was crucified when he was thirty-three. And I can't sleep. Sometimes.'

'Why do you want Temazepam?'

'I've had it before at Easter. When I can't sleep.'

'Are you . . . tired?'

'Oh no.' He wasn't making any effort to disguise the fact that he was reading. One doctor's interesting case is another doctor's basketcase. 'Well, I am tired – when I can't sleep. At the moment I feel OK. But maybe later I'll have insomnia and it's reassuring to know that the tablets are there just in case.'

It's years since I've had to explain myself like this. Don't I sound convincing? Or is Dr Hope just impossible to impress.

'Temazepam is a powerful drug.'

'Only when it's injected.'

'Do you . . . inject?'

'I've seen it on TV.'

'Why not just have a glass of milk when you can't sleep.'

'I've never liked milk. Anyway, it's bad for the digestion.'

'I beg to differ,' he said. 'Milk always works for me.' Judging from the bags under his eyes, Dr Hope looks like he hasn't slept since the sixties. But I buttoned my lip, smiling vaguely, the way you do when someone you can't stand makes a beeline for you at a party.

He broke our silence by asking, 'What do you think about when you can't sleep?'

'Depends.' Stupidity's a powerful weapon. He's wearing me out.

'Do you think about death?'

'Sometimes. Usually I make lists in my head of things I want or need. A new pack of Camay soap, a helicopter, another pair of black boots.'

'I see.' Dr Grant would ask how many pairs of boots I have, perhaps glancing, more seductive than lecherous, at my feet. Maybe we'd discuss Catherine Deneuve, a well-known shoe fetishist. Dr Hope monotones on, 'When did you first become aware of . . . suicide?'

'Suicide? Who knows. I was quite young when I saw *Waterloo Bridge*. Then Sarah kills herself in *The Hustler*. That's always been one of my favourite movies. You don't actually see it happening. Does she swallow pills or slash her wrists? And you don't see Vivien Leigh jumping into the Thames either. Charlie Castle slashes his wrists off camera in *The Big Knife*. You know because he's in the bath and it's an honour thing. I've been mad about that movie for years. You can feel the blood drip through the ceiling as Ida Lupino raises her eyes in God's direction.'

'You have a close relationship with this fantasy world?'

'Look,' I said, 'I'd love to chat, but I have another appointment.'

'I don't want to keep you.'

'Could I have my prescription?' I'm already almost sure that Dr Hope would rather kill himself than give me my jellies. Though I'm certainly not going to discuss John with him. He knows already anyway.

'When did you first become aware of death?' Maybe he's testing me? Trying to see if my answers are the same as they were for Dr Grant. That's it, he's a truth hound.

'Well,' I said, sitting up straight. 'I don't know exactly but it was way before my grandfather died. The day before I went into hospital I remember being really worried about a yellow rose in my mother's handbag. I was terrified it was going to die before we got home from the park. I kept asking her to open the bag and make sure it was still alive.'

'How old were you then?'

'Two.'

'Why were you hospitalized?'

'Tonsils. Maddie was a hygiene fanatic and it was a dead fashionable op in the sixties.' As my face moved from side to side, avoiding the gas, other children including my brother lay comatose on queasy green rows of operating tables.

'Your mother?'

'Yes. She took me to the park to explain that putting me in the hospital didn't mean that she hated my guts.'

'And the rose?'

'She stole it.'

'Your mother stole a rose from the public park?'

'Yes, a yellow rose. She could have bought me a bunch, but I really liked the look of that particular rose. I worried all the way home that it was going to suffocate. But when we got back it was still alive and I put it in a bowl by my bed. When I got out of hospital the rose was gone.'

'It had died.'

'No, she'd thrown it in the bin. Its petals were going every-where. She thought I'd have forgotten about it, and anyway, she could just steal me another one next time we went to the park. But I only liked that rose. And I'd wanted to keep its petals in my bible.'

'Were you upset?'

'I was angry.'

'What did you do?'

'I waited until she wasn't expecting it. Then, when we were out shopping, I leaped out of my pram outside Fraser's and took a stick to her leg. Her flesh-coloured nylons were ripped to bits and there was blood. So she says; I can't remember exactly.'

'Was this Fraser a . . . friend . . . of your mother's?'

'No, it's a shop. House of Fraser. Glasgow's Harrods.'

'Were there other . . . acts of violence?'

'Mainly verbal violence. I'd threaten to kill myself if she didn't do what I wanted. Or say, "I hope you die and get eaten by a dog." '

'Mainly?'

'Sometimes I dug my nails into her.'

'Did you draw blood?'

'How would I know?'

'Did your mother behave violently towards you?'

'Are you kidding? She used to beat my brother up with her shoe but she never touched me, I'm a girl.' Dr Hope was wondering if I was winding him up. If I was a doctor, I'd refuse to see narcissistic nuts. But I'm the patient. He's being paid. He isn't even my doctor! Oh yes, it's my appointment and I can be self-indulgent if I want to.

'Tell me about the . . . tubercular toe.'

'Dangerous calls it my immaculate consumption – the germs passed straight to my toe leaving no shadow on my lung.' I'd always wanted to be consumptive – pale, frail and dangerous to kiss – like Emily Brontë, rumoured to have died of love for her weak brother Branwell.

'Was Dangerous your doctor?'

'My husband.'

'May I examine . . . the toe?'

'Certainly not.'

'I promise not to touch, just look.' Nosy fucking parker!

'There's nothing to see. It did go green for a while but it's white again now.'

'You were prescribed sleeping tablets?'

'Yes but I didn't take them. I stayed up all night watching movies.'

'Afraid to sleep in case you would die?'

'Enjoying myself. Susan Sontag got it wrong. Illness definitely is metaphor. Jane Bowles and Bernadette of Lourdes had tubercular legs. For me, the TB toe was the perfect illness. Although I don't think Jennifer Jones should have played St Bernadette in the movie, do you? Everyone associates her with *Lust in the Dust*. And if you really want to know everything, I think Bernadette's a rotten name for a saint. Not sexy enough.'

'You were hospitalized?'

'Briefly, like it says in the file.' Because there was no shadow on my lung, the chest clinic didn't want me after the biopsy. The Orthopaedic ward was packed with amputees who kept staring at my bandages, wondering what was missing. In the middle of the night, while the nurse was on the phone to her boyfriend, I limped out and stopped a taxi, desperate to get back to my empty flat to unravel the stained bandages and make sure my green toe was still there.

'Do you associate hospitals with abandonment?'

'I love hospitals! I met my husband in the elevator at UCH. He gave me seven yellow roses he was taking to his dying grandmother.' Sylvia Plath's corpse was taken to UCH for examination. Why gas yourself when you have a drawer full of sleeping tablets? Imagine, sticking your head in an oven! No matter how vigorous the housewife, there's bound to be a greasy ming. It's a macabre touch, in a family apparently obsessed with birds, that she laid her head in the spot usually occupied by a chicken.

'You knew each other?'

'I'd seen his picture in a magazine. He recognized my walking-stick and said, "You're the girl with the tubercular toe!" I was famous in the hospital. No one else in this country has ever had a tubercular toe.'

'Certainly, there are no recorded cases,' he glanced up for a second, 'other than yours.'

'I have to see Darren in seven minutes. His salon's quite near here.' I stood up, put on my gloves.

'I'm afraid I can't prescribe sleeping tablets . . . without further investigation.' They're not even real sleeping pills!

'Oh well,' I said. 'I'll buy a couple of extra bottles of Stolichnaya.'

As I walked south towards Mayfair, carefully avoiding collision with traffic, I knew that even without John – a rock solid destructive chic excuse – I'd still get morbid sometimes. Feeling

like death every Easter could just be a bad habit, or a good habit
– a useful purge, like Lent.

A fire engine rattled past as I crossed Oxford Street, annoying
the taxis, buses and anxious shoppers. Memories exist in the
present tense. I don't know if the Kelly babies burned to death
in their beds before or after I lost my tonsils. In my mind,
it's my first memory of death: sudden, dramatic, forbidden.
Everyone went quiet when their mother came into the sweetie
shop. After she'd left with a brightly coloured selection from
the penny tray, Old Wilma behind the counter said to Maddie,
'It was suicidal – her leaving them alone like that.'

Everyone has two childhoods: the ecstatic and the desperate.
Each version is jumbled together in technicolour, chiaroscuro,
violence and excitement.

Hitchcock Blonde

Hairdressers are always called Darren or Sharon, Nicki or Vicki. If they're not they should be. They slave all day in shops without windows, for hundred note tips, because a good haircut changes your life, and a bad one is too painful to think about.

The thrilling artificially lit interior of Darren's shop reminds me of a night out in a traditional cinema. Skinny black and white boys and girls deliver plates of chips and cans of Superblow to women draped in towels and stylists in tight trousers.

You used to be able to buy a bag of chips and take them into the Rio. The staff didn't care if you dropped a handful laced in ketchup. Concealed in your seat, there was already a used condom and a family of fleas. A big cat chased the cinema rats around the darkness as the smell of salt and vinegar made the movie more fun.

'Blonde?' Darren asked. 'You mean fair?'

'Blonde,' I said. 'Harlow blonde. Hitchcock blonde. Heathen blonde.'

'You mean ash?'

'Blonde blonde. White can't-miss-it blonde. Marilyn Monroe on her deathbed. Sylvia Plath during the peroxide summer. Kim

Novak in *Vertigo*. Tippi Hedren in *Marnie*. Kelly the prostitute in *Naked Kiss*. Jean Harlow in her coffin.'

'There's a rumour,' Darren said slowly, 'in hairdressing circles, that Harlow died of peroxide poisoning.' Our eyes met briefly in the mirror, before Darren switched the scrutiny of his gaze back to his own slender figure. 'She was only twenty-six when she died.'

'Well,' I said, 'definitely no middle-aged-woman yellow, labrador gold, swimming-pool green, or OAP blue.' Everything I've ever seen in the movies blonde.

'Black's in this month.'

'Fashion fades, style stays.'

'OK, Miss Blonde, do you want a double espresso before we start? A champagne-tequila?'

'A glass of sparkling ice water, no lemon.'

As I waited for Darren to come back with the bottle of bleach, I felt my will draining away. Sitting there is better than praying. Without suffering the sore knees of Mass, my brain falls into a luxurious coma. Darren could stick his Japanese scissors in my eye and I wouldn't feel a thrill, even though they're the sharpest and most expensive in the world. They're sitting beside his bust of Plato on the counter, waiting to destroy my split ends.

According to Maddie, I stabbed a hairdresser 'somewhere in Mayfair' when I was two. We were shopping in London, living at the Ritz, and she took me to a really posh place for an Emma Peel. The result was more Dennis the Menace. Maddie's punchline is always, 'When she saw herself in the mirror the wee one jumped out of her high chair and flew at the woman with a pair of scissors. Then the manager begged us to leave without paying.'

Today in the mirror my skin is pale and exciting as it waits for its blonde halo. The thick make-up of Hollywood heroines gleaming white under the key lights encouraged me to grow up with an expectation of perfect skin.

Judd the Junior brought me a pile of magazines with my drink. Darren came back with an alarming big ear-to-ear grin and a dish of smelly stuff. A little Vaseline to protect my hairline and Hey Presto, 'We're really going to do this,' he said, slopping some on to my hair.

Now, we only have to sit nice waiting for the transformation.

Hitchcock's women all wear the same suit.

The sexy grey of Kim's in *Vertigo*, the sleeveless green dress Tippi wears in *The Birds* are identical only in my memory. When you examine the movies, there's a relationship between the elegant tailoring but not the colour or style.

I'm paying my bill, everyone's gushing over me, saying how much like a movie star I look in my curaçao suit – set off by my gleaming blonde hair – and I feel happiness reaching out to me, the way it does in the dark when I'm watching a movie alone, wishing I was the only one in the auditorium. Oh yes, I could be happy.

'It's a miracle,' Darren says, like a decadent God, watching me.

Out in the street, I had a craving for a newspaper but couldn't see a man selling them. Suddenly no taxis, and I'm late for my skin perfecting appointment.

Running in my high heels, I see The Future The Future . . . leaping ahead of me, defying death.

Thursday

Each of Maddie's old flat feet is steeped in a porcelain bowl of hot water scented with Chanel.

'My daughter,' she told the Japanese DKNY assistant this afternoon, 'has not inherited my feet. Forced me to bandage them when she was wee so that she wouldn't end up with big boats like mine.' The girl smiled without replying all the way to the cash register with my high-heeled slingbacks, satin boots and patent leather courts.

'My God,' she says, 'I can't get over you blonde.' She's been saying that since I surprised her at the airport this morning with my Harlow-white hair. 'It really sets off your face.' She can't resist adding, 'You look less like him now and more like me.'

It's almost seven. The French clock on the marble mantelpiece of her Louis-Seize suite is about to strike. 'Tomorrow's the big day,' I say.

'I know that.'

'I wasn't sure if you remembered.'

'I'm not senile! Friday's the only night Jonathan can make dinner. He's a busy man, you know. It's just as well you turned

145

up at the airport this morning or I would have been stranded with him having to buzz over to France like that. Give me a tumbler of brandy, will you.' I pour Grand Marnier into a glass, stumbling into Manhattan skyline shoe boxes and Bond Street tissue wrap as I weave my way towards her. 'Good for my dodgy heart,' she says, gulping it back as soon as I hand it to her.

The Ritz clock chimes seven times on cue. I go through to the dressing room, hanging up my new black Chanel dress alongside the ludicrous pink satin creation she insisted on buying as well to go with my lively new look. 'You are going to stay the night?' she calls through the open door. 'My doctor doesn't think it would be good for me to be alone. Try your dress on again and let me see you in it.'

When I go out she tuts, 'It should have been made-to-measure. And I wish you'd stop harping on about him, I'm sick to death of the subject. Anyway, Easter's on a different date every year, you know. They move it around. Your brother's little drama could have been last week for all you know.'

'Don't be ridiculous. You know it's his birthday to-morrow.'

'Ha!' She raises her glass as if she's about to slash me with it. 'Why would he want to kill himself on his birthday of all days.'

'You know fine and well he did it on his birthday for symmetrical reasons. Stop pretending to be thicker than you are.'

'You have to be suspicious of people with perfect memories,' she says, doubling her chin defiantly into her neck.

'You look like your sad sister when you do that.'

'Which one?' she cackles. 'What would you like for your

birthday? Dangerous and you could both come to L.A. with us. It would be great!'

'I'd like to go to New York.'

'You would. Mark my words, you'll end up murdered one of these days.'

Later, when we were sitting nice in our satin pyjamas, she says, 'I don't understand you. Why can't you visit me? It's much nicer than New York. I'll rent you a car.' Even though I can't wait for tonight to be over with, am dreading the bit at bedtime when she removes her front falsies, and having to lie there in the dark listening to her snore, part of me dreads never seeing her again.

'You know I can't stand the sun.' And part of me dreads knowing we will meet again! She'll make sure of it.

'You were always a wee queer hawk,' she says, as the Spanish waiter brings in the supper snacks. The bent man lugs the table of smoked salmon, oysters, and tiger prawns (a protein overdose guaranteed to keep me awake, thanks to Dr fucking Hope) over to where we sit.

'Rub some of that extortionate cream into my old feet,' Maddie says.

'Certainly, Mrs Money,' he says, kneeling down.

'Oh not you, Mr Semolina. I was talking to my daughter.' That can't be his name, but neither of them acknowledge the possibility of a mistake. 'Do you remember my daughter? Looks different now that she's a blonde.'

'Of course,' Mr Semolina grins at me. 'How are you, Miss Money?'

'Mrs Watson these days,' I reply, spoiling the fun.

'Once a Money always a Money,' he says, trivial yet profound.

'Is this the suite Judy Garland stayed in?'

'The two suites on this floor are the best in the hotel,' he says.

'But was she in this one or the other one?'

'We'd have to check the records. When was Miss Garland here?'

'1968.'

'Ah. I was in Spain in '68.' He looks like he might be about to make an interesting confession.

'Ignore her, Mr Semolina. My daughter is a queer hawk.' Señor Semolina collects his tip and makes his exit, promising to 'see us later'.

'Such a nice man,' Maddie says.

'How much did you tip him?'

'Nothing for nosy folk.'

'Mr Pink never tips.'

'Who in Hell's name is Mr Pink?'

'In *Reservoir Dogs*.'

'I might have known. Well Mr Pink's got it wrong. You tip when you're going to see the person again, to buy loyalty. Where are you off to now?'

'I'm flying to Tokyo with a black man I met in the elevator this afternoon.'

'I don't know where you get it from.'

In her marble bathroom, the phone rings. Cool water from the gold taps washes over my wrists as I consider listening in. But eavesdropping on her conversation with Jonathan would be obscene. I'll find out tomorrow night whether she drubs him or takes the coy sheep approach.

Picking up her vanity scissors, I snip a split end off my white hair. Monsieur Darrendo missed that one all right. Or has it grown since yesterday? Growth is almost as sinister as decay.

Sitting on the floor, enjoying the touch of the cold marble tiles, time flies.

'What are you up to in there?' she shouts.

'Giving myself a shot of morphine.'

'You don't improve with age,' she says, slapping me across the head when I resume my place on the sofa. And, glaring at my rosary, 'Your grandfather's turning in his grave right now. Why on earth do you have to wear that thing with your pyjamas?' The sisters are still dead embarrassed about my conversion to Catholicism. If they ever find out about my tubercular toe, Maddie will have to slash her wrists. When they were wee, only poor folk were afflicted with both diseases. Her big mouth opens, sucking in the last oyster. She still has her tonsils. Truly terrifying. 'He only did it to spite you. He was dead selfish.' Her eyes are hard and ugly. Old women have a knack for looking cold or disappointed.

'Shall we call downstairs and see what videos they've got?'

'Maybe they'd make us popcorn!'

'I'm sure Mr Semolina would love to make you popcorn,' she laughs. Her laughter reminds me she's not the full banana, though I hadn't forgotten.

As we're waiting for *An Affair to Remember*, and the air-popped corn, she says, 'I was dead jealous of the two of you the night you went to see Gary Glitter. If it hadn't been for him you would have let me go.'

'You didn't have to come with us.'

'It's not the same going on your own. None of my sisters were interested.' Her legs whiff of fake tan. 'He was creepy. Like that Richard Carpenter.'

'Gary Glitter?'

'No, that brother of yours!'

'John looks nothing like Richard Carpenter,' I say, outraged.

'But the Carpenters fancied each other, didn't they? He was always giving you funny looks. You had a narrow escape with that one.' Her smile gives me the creeps.

Good Friday

The Ritz clock announces midnight.

Good Friday. Today's the day. My Fortnum's Easter egg – blue foil with a silver ribbon – is waiting at the bottom of my bed where she used to put our birthday presents. Leaving Maddie asleep, I pick up the egg and tiptoe through the dressing room into the living room.

Outside, Piccadilly is still thick with traffic but Green Park's deserted. Dumping the egg, I climb on to the balcony in my bare feet, enjoying the breeze fluttering up my jammie legs.

Trees are your complexion's best friend. They breathe in all the bad air, converting it into pure stuff. Looking down, I feel dizzy even though I'm not up that high. High enough. Roughly the same height as the slate roof of our building in Glasgow.

'Why don't you?' Mrs Danvers asks in *Rebecca*. She's talking to Joan Fontaine, the new Mrs de Winter, but really she's talking to me and you. 'It's easy. Go on. Don't be afraid.'

John died today. And last year. And next year. Someday I'll die, but not today. I'm dead scared. If I kill myself, I'm betraying Dangerous. Loving one person usually makes you feel disloyal to another.

*   *   *

John had always wanted to destroy himself. Walking to school in the morning, we stared at the sun. One day I asked, 'Why do we do this?'

'To make us go blind,' he said. I bought my first shades from Johnnie's toy and sweetie shop – white plastic Lolita sunnies, we were inseparable until the blue mirrors of early punk.

On the way home, I hugged the edges of the tenements hiding from the wind. He swayed off the pavement into the traffic, praying to be run over. 'You could push me when I least expect it,' he said when I stopped to tie my shoelace.

Every year, on this night, the speed of years becomes the sloth of minutes. The usual time tricks don't work in the dark. Switching on the TV, I take a bite of my Easter egg, but my heart's not in it. Though I'm in luck, *Butterfield 8*'s on.

Butterfield 8 is a funny name for a telephone exchange. Hollywood's the master of queer hawk names. Gloria Wandrous is such a stupid name for a slut-girl, it's perfect. There was a Liz Taylor – call me Elizabeth – in our class at school. She looked nothing like the real Liz.

I've missed the beginning, but I know the story. You have to fall in love with this movie before you're nine, otherwise you agree with Liz Taylor's verdict: 'It's a piece of trash.' Even as a teenager, you're too old for the flab spilling out of her slip as she stumbles around Laurence Harvey's bedroom. But there's the Hollywood phallic bit with the shoe to look forward to, when she stabs him with her stiletto.

The bloated colour face of Gloria Wandrous is only seven years older than the perfect black and white face of Angela Vickers. Elizabeth's spent too much time at that place in the sun. And Gloria's lips aren't red! If a slut doesn't wear Firebrand she shouldn't have lipstick at all. Liz's thin mouth is coated with

152

orangey paint – a technicolour betrayal of the scarlet illusion of noir.

John went out on a date with a nurse called Liz, a girl with dyed black hair that looked as if it was only washed once a week. Too thin to resemble SuperLiz, she had the big beezers anyway. They had drinks first then went to a movie. He was sulking because they'd split for the drinks and the tickets, but his drink was cheaper than hers. Afterwards, she said she didn't like the movie.

They drove to her house in silence until he asked, 'Have you ever seen a dead body?'

'No,' she admitted.

'Any amputations?'

'You're weird,' she said, staring at the light in her parents' living room window.

Later he came into my room, sitting on the end of my bed. 'Did you kiss her?' I asked.

'Are you kidding? She hated *Blood for Dracula!*' Sex and death and humour, one of our favourite movies.

'I don't know why you took her to see it anyway.'

'I didn't take her.'

'You went with her.'

He stared straight ahead, watching his shirt buttons in the mirror. 'Do you want to see?'

'No.'

He unbuttoned the white cotton shirt he'd ironed himself. Across his chest, deep Kung Fu gashes were still weeping.

'Good night,' I said, killing the light.

One thirty-one and all's not well. You can make yourself older by moving the hands of your watch or younger by altering the date on your passport. Time stops when you're engrossed in a movie. It doesn't matter when you're happy and matters too much when you're dwelling on your own wee tragedy.

John died seven years ago, everyone's lucky number.

It was the day I couldn't find a tube of Firebrand. London was exploding with tourists that spring. Spring is the favourite season for suicide. I walked from my building to Selfridges with the crumbly remains of my lipstick in my pocket, confident of replacing it.

Out of all the reds I could be addicted to – Russian Red, VivaGlam, Rouge Imaginaire, Number 36, Perfect Silent Red – I've always been secretly in love with the matt perfection of the cheap, plastic Firebrand.

Department stores in Glasgow sell the tack stuff alongside the perfectly-packaged products. All the best colours are cheap and dangerous. But Selfridges don't have a Max Factor counter.

'Don't they have air conditioning in here?' I asked the Estée Lauder tart. She rolled her eyes in sympathy or disgust. Sometimes it's hard to tell.

Heart hurting, I had to get to Boots immediately. Crossing Oxford Street, I lunged into the slow traffic – determined, aggressive. The small branch by Bond Street station didn't have any Firebrands left. I took a cab to Piccadilly, but was too nervous to stay in it the whole journey. Jumping out in Regent Street, I didn't wait for my change, and actually ran to Piccadilly Circus. People were looking at me like I was a lunatic.

'Have you got a Firebrand?' I spat saliva nervously at the assistant, the way Maddie does when talking to people she can't stand – 'sharing germs generously'.

'That's been discontinued,' she said, casually turning to a woman who wanted to pay for a liquid eyeliner. Why would they discontinue it? They're always doing things like that. Resurrecting old shades with a new name, so you have to search and search and, when you find it, wonder for ages if it's an *exact* copy or just close. But Firebrand's been around for fifty years. Same name, same colour.

'Have you any old stock?'

'Old stock?'

'I'm wearing Firebrand,' the girl from the Seventeen counter shouted across the aisle. Good for you, bitch. Too bad you put the lipgloss on top, ruining the total look. 'There's loads of them in the box by the till.'

The lazy girl who'd lied to me bent reluctantly to fetch one. 'I thought you meant Firebird,' she said, handing me my colour to inspect. A likely story.

'I've never heard of Firebird.'

'An orangey shade,' she persisted.

'I'll take seven Firebrands,' I said.

'Seven?' she asked, tossing them into a paperbag, demanding the money with a sour smile. Our fingers touched as she threw the change into my palm.

Maddie calls while I'm ironing my Agnes B silk shirt, Firebrand tattooed over my lips, the Channel 4 news on as background music. Through the urban glamour of current affairs, I can't make out what she's saying.

'He just went flying past the window!'

'What?' Her voice is more hysterical than usual.

'Thank God for the witness – it would be just like him to make it look like I shoved him.'

'What are you talking about?'

'That brother of yours. He's just jumped off the roof.'

'Is he dead?'

*　　*　　*

155

The jewel-encrusted Louis-Seize clock chimes three times. Three used to be one of my numbers. Now it's common and useless. You can change your mind about a number the way you do about a person. Even seven — my all-time favourite — is wearing out from too much significance.

Gulping back some Stolichnaya, I wondered if I should clean my teeth again?

Maddie was outraged when I called back to say I'd arrive at seven in the morning.

'You would have to be in London at a time like this,' she said. 'Why can't you fly?'

'The last flight's gone.'

'I don't believe you,' she said, absurd.

'Do you think I want to sit up all night on the fucking train?'

It was the last train before Good Friday. The seats were all booked, I had to stand by the toilet. People stared at my cartoon lips and manic smile. All through the night, I locked myself in the toilet, washed my hands, got bored, went back out.

A heart-attack corpse was taken off the train at Newcastle. The medical student who had tried to revive it stood crying by the stretcher as two paramedics manoeuvred it out the door.

'His wife's going to have to pick him up,' the aspiring doctor said to me.

Details flashed through my mind like the dream sequence in *Spellbound*. When did I last have my legs waxed? Two stiff cold black-clad legs. Can't examine their smooth finish until they're naked.

'Your legs,' John told me, 'are like plastic. I keep expecting you to take them off and hang them up.'

My first suicide! God forgive me – a quick Hail Mary for vanity. A boy who fancied me at school tried to slash his wrists. 'It's dead romantic,' Lolita said. His name was John, too. But an unsuccessful suicide isn't the same. I wanted to grow up and live in a white mansion, wearing Firebrand even for breakfast, and have millions of men committing suicide over me.

Is God watching? A bout of hysteria was quelled by the sight of two teenagers tonguing each other.

'Hope your mum's bought you a rotten Easter egg!' I shouted, startling everyone including myself.

The Clarins Natural Brown lip pencil is long and elegant and equally effective for lining the eyes. Scissors are dignified and hammers are dangerous. Seven times seven is forty-nine. I'm dizzy with hunger but can't eat.

Sylvia Plath sounds like a bore. I heard her voice on a radio recording. I've always hated her big flabby face. Somewhere between the overweight faces of the middle aged and the slack cheeks of youth.

Marilyn Monroe wore her bra to bed. Sid Vicious was a joke. Jim Morrison got fat. Ian Curtis reminds me of my heavy silver hairbrush because I was disinfecting it when John ran into the bathroom shouting, 'Ian Curtis hung himself!'

The local papers in the station kiosk had John's photograph on the front.

MONEY HEIR FALLS FROM ROOF.

'That's a laugh,' Maddie said, marching up to me, 'he's never been in my will in his life.' I picked a newspaper up without paying for it. He's Montgomery Clift with a love hangover and I'm definitely not Elizabeth Taylor.

Maddie pushed her way to the front of the taxi queue. 'Keep

that thing out of sight! What will folk be saying?' Out of the
corner of her mouth, she asked, 'What will I do?

'Emigrate?'

'That's not a bad idea. I'll get the blame for this, you know.
It's always the mother's fault.'

'You mean you didn't push him?'

'Don't get smart today of all days and what is that you have
on your mouth?'

'Firebrand.'

'Couldn't you give Sugar Pink a try? What will folk think if
you go around looking like a Jezebel at a time like this.' She
used to call me a wee Firebrand, a wee Jezebel, a nasty wee
bitch, a wee angel, a cheeky devil, a special wee thing, a wee
nutcase. Identity problem.

Maddie barged into the first taxi that pulled up, ignoring
the muttering queue ahead of us. Her skirt rode too far up
her thighs. She couldn't be bothered fixing it. Legs crossed,
she told me, 'You'll have to do something. I want him down
the hatch straight after the inquest, but the undertakers are
all shut for Good Friday. I just want this over and done with.'
She covered her face with her hands, eyes peeping out at
the top.

'Don't you dare,' I warned. 'I'm not in the mood for hys-
terics.'

Her face went scarlet. Suddenly switching to a normal voice,
she said, 'I need a new pair of shoes for the funeral and so do
you by the looks of things.'

'You have millions of shoes,' I said, sounding like her, 'and
the shops are shut.'

'Tomorrow's another day,' she answered back.

'Where did they get the photograph?'

'What photograph?'

'The photograph of John. In the paper.' She shrugged, going red. 'You didn't sell it?'

'Not me!'

The taxi pulled up outside our building. Seeing it always cheers me up, God knows why. 'It was your Auntie Vagina,' Maddie said. 'She did it.'

'I've always loathed that woman.'

Maddie giggled. 'The feeling's mutual, I can assure you.' She paid the driver, unable to resist giving him a flirty smile.

'You look familiar,' he said. 'Are you a film star or something?'

'People say I could have been,' she said, piling on the tip. 'When I was young I was the double of that Grace Kelly.'

Maddie was too mortified to call the man who arranged the disposal of Grandfather Money's remains, and all the dead Moneys before him. But it was impossible to find another under-taker who was willing to burn John on Easter Sunday at such short notice. Eventually I had to call Mr Priceless.

'I'll have to charge you double,' Mr Priceless said when we went to see him on Saturday morning. He didn't recognize us or pretended not to. I knew him right away. Middle-aged faces don't change to the onlooker, only to the man observing himself in the mirror. John and I were at school with his daughter, Barbie. She used to borrow the hearse at weekends to drive into town. One time her and John ended up in the hearse alone and she kissed him.

'It was terrifying,' he said, when reporting back later. 'Her mouth was like the sponge Vagina and Penis use to clean their bath.'

'I can't believe you allowed tongues.'

'I didn't. She forced hers into my mouth. Practically broke my teeth.'

'Yuk,' I said.

'There's no way I'm putting an ad in the evening paper,' Maddie told Mr Priceless, whose name is really Bob Price: Funeral Director. Bob's your burner, not your uncle. Boom, boom.

'It isn't compulsory,' he said, 'just bear in mind I can get you a discount.'

'I have to take my daughter for a decent pair of shoes before the inquest,' she said. 'Phew, it's all go.' I've seen an inquest on *Rebecca*. The idea of them all talking about him turns my stomach. But it doesn't seem real. It's still out there in the imaginary future, even though it's happening this afternoon. 'Of course it's a clear-cut case,' Maddie had said on the phone to Grandfather's lawyer. 'There's not much left of him to examine.' Splat! Bang! Pow! Squashed on the pavement like Mickey Mouse, without getting up to finish the cartoon.

'See you tomorrow, Mrs Money,' Mr Priceless said, adding stagily, 'at the Garden of Death.' Or was it Fountain of Remembrance? Something like that.

Trying on a pair of black patent leather pumps with a square but elegant heel, I asked, 'Why don't you ever correct anyone when they call you Mrs Money?'

'My father and I were very close.' She shrugged. 'Thank God your grandfather's name still means something in this town.' When we went on the inheritance tour, she always registered us as 'Mrs Money and her daughter Maria'. It made her feel dead rich, dead cool, dead glamorous.

'What do you mean close?'

'Don't be ridiculous! It's a nice name, that's all. Anyway,' she added, as if the John dialogue had never been interrupted, 'he didn't have friends, who'd notice if I put an ad in?'

John had been the popular boy at school. By the time I came back from New York, he'd gone funny. 'What's the point?' he asked, when I suggested us sharing a flat in London. He came to see me in King's Cross without phoning in advance. The sight of him, clean and sane, reassured me. Not being able to remember someone's face is a sign of love. Love is for the very young – as Lana Turner says in *The Bad and Beautiful*. John's good looks always shocked me.

Maddie was stressing about the time but we dodged into Fraser's for a quick cup of tea. Past the perfume counters, up the stairs, she kept glaring at her watch – a crocodile-strap Cartier inlaid with thirteen diamonds. While she stopped to eye up a canary yellow suit with black lace trim – the sort of get-up Carmen would wear to a job interview – I checked that my keys and money and spare scissors and passport were in my bag. Leaving my passport at home makes me nervous even when I'm not planning to defect to Berlin.

Laughter came out of her even though no one had told a joke as we sat in a booth together, her with an Earl Grey, me with a gut-turning hot chocolate. Since yesterday morning we'd been together constantly. In the middle of the night she even came into my room while I was lying making a list of all my favourite movies with a suicide in them.

'You asleep?' she whispered, the way she used to do in Grand Hotels.

'Yes.'

'You are not, you just spoke.'

161

'Go away.'

'Let's see what's on the telly?' she pleaded.

All the way through my video of *A Place in the Sun* she went on and on about how it was 'for the best'.

'He'd never have made anything of himself.'

An old bat wearing a hat like a chocolate layer cake sat next to us.

'We'd better rush,' Maddie said, giving the old idiot one of her *noblesse oblige* smiles. 'You can't keep a man in a wig waiting.'

'A coroner doesn't wear a wig unless he's bald. I'll be back in a minute,' I said.

'I'll come with you.'

'No – watch the bags.'

The toilet attendant interrupted me with a story about a dead body she'd found locked in one of the stalls.

'How did you get the door open?' I asked.

'Bert from Maintenance had to bash it in.'

'How did you know there was a corpse in there?'

'Are you kidding? I could tell from the stink. Anyway, I looked under the door and saw it sitting there.'

'It could just have been someone with constipation,' I persisted, running cold water on my wrists.

'No, it was dead exciting,' the attendant said, glancing at her dyed black bouffant hair in the mirror.

'Who was the woman?'

'I never asked her!' Boom, boom. 'I can't mind her name, but it definitely happened ten years ago to this day though. My cat, Wetty, had just died.' Ten years! She made it sound like yesterday. Death's a memorable drama. It's her own macabre anecdote. Nothing's happened in this toilet since.

'A lot of things happened that year,' I said, avoiding the soap but enjoying the water running over my fingers. She looked at me like I'm the ultimate queer hawk, but was still eager to keep the conversation going.

'That cat was irreplaceable.'

'You've been working here ten years?' I asked, drying my hands.

'Fifteen,' she said casually, staring at her tip saucer. My concentration was poor. The inquest was going to be nothing compared with the funeral. I've never been to a burning before and can't even imagine it, even though I've seen many on TV. This time, there'd be no adverts and the body being consumed was his. Tomorrow there will be no way out of here. Public transport is fucked up on Jesus's big day, and I can't drive when I'm desperate. The pound coin I put in her tip saucer looked lost sitting there.

'Ta,' she said. She must have told that corpse story a million times. Maybe she made it up to make her work sound interesting? 'You're like a young Elizabeth Taylor,' she went on, sucking up. 'Folk said that about me years ago.'

'Thanks a lot. Hey, can you think of the names of any movies when someone gets burnt?'

'Huh?' The only example I can come up with, at short notice, is *The Wicker Man*. And that's an unusual funeral. The actor is burned in the open air, with a bunch of extras dancing round him. Well, it's the Highlands.

The sisters and everybody were going to be there. Lolita may even turn up. I'm already cast as chief mourner, devoted daughter, distraught sister, but this time I'm not going to live down to the audience's expectations.

Running, I reached Central Station on time for the one o'clock train. The Flying Scotsman had a seat for me – a good omen – and when I got back to my flat in King's Cross everything had been stolen. Even the furniture. The phone was gone, I couldn't call the police. Better still, the sisters couldn't call me screaming, 'How could you?!'

This empty new flat was thrilling even though the holy trinity of heavy hammer, good scissors and wee gun were missing from my bedside along with the bed. Insides of drawers were strewn over the floor, papers and books and fishnet stockings the thieves didn't want, and when I sat down beside them I found the day's post in a tidy pile behind the damaged door.

John's letter said, *Drinking Stolichnaya in Heaven maybe, dreaming of you.*

Straight away, before I lost my nerve, I crawled around the floor until I found my bag, took the travelling scissors out and cut the paper and cut it and cut it until it didn't exist. Taking off my silly shoe, I threw it at the mirror, daring it to give me seven years' bad luck. Glass jumped all over the place without managing to hit me.

Of course I kept the locket that was also in the envelope. I couldn't get it to open. Sometimes a strand of hair pushes its way out between the hinges.

When I got around to calling the police, they were outraged: 'We've never seen anything like it,' the two constables kept saying. 'Usually they just take the video and the computer.'

The youngest PC went into the kitchen and came back alarmed, 'They've even taken the tea bags!'

'Well,' I said. 'Junkies. Pimps. Pushers. Bad-tempered commuters. Some day a real rain's unlikely to come.'

*　　*　　*

Back in the Ritz bedroom, Maddie's still snoring. That woman can sleep through anything.

Disobeying her, I opened the window.

'Someone will climb in and murder us in our beds if you open that thing. I don't care what floor we're on! They all have ladders . . .'

Taking another gulp of Russian vodka, I lay on my bed – falling.

Naked Kiss

In the afternoon when I stumbled out, Maddie's Louis-Seize living room had the distinctive scent of smoke.

Upturned on her gilt sofa, there's a book about Ruth Ellis who has glamour written all over her pencilled eyebrows. Her timing was perfect, she murdered her boyfriend on Easter Sunday; and was rewarded with the role of peroxide angel. Her broken neck and broken heart are inseparable. Now the daughter's trading her bad blood for a cash advance. The son hanged himself.

Maddie, on her knees in front of her mini-bar, said over her shoulder, 'That book's a right laugh.' My mother's a biography hound who only barks for dirt, a voyeuristic trait we share. 'My God, your eyes are like bullet holes. Put some make-up on for God's sake.'

'Have you been smoking?'

'Not full time,' she said, smelling her fingers.

'Death's the cure for all diseases.'

'Let's go out on the balcony,' she replied, 'if you're going to get morbid.'

Below in Green Park, pink people sprawled in peppermint deck chairs. Hot cars trailed along Piccadilly. You can never trust the weather in London. Tomorrow it could be freezing.

'Devil's spawn,' Maddie said as a giant fly, dressed by Balenciaga, landed on the ice bucket. She ignored the wine, pouring herself a big tumbler of brandy. 'Of course I don't enjoy drinking, I only do it for the sake of my heart. Don't suppose you want one, sober sides?'

'Certainly not.' I'm not one of those social drinkers. I drink alone, or with my husband, and I definitely enjoy it. I'm full of praise for the power of champagne, chablis, cassis. Better for the heart than heroin, cheaper too. Legal, accessible, painless.

'Today's the day,' I said.

'We had this conversation yesterday. I'm hardly likely to forget. Like I said, this is the only night Jon could make dinner. He's a busy man, you know. Have you thought any more about your birthday? As if I haven't bought you enough already!'

'Like I said, I want to go to New York.'

'You've been there millions of times! You went to school there, for God's sake. It's about time you gave some other place a try. Mark my words, you'll end up murdered one of these days.' After being seduced by something in a movie you're supposed to be disappointed when you experience it in real life. New York City isn't like that. Being there is just as real as imagining it. When I'm a real gloom-balloon, more suicidal than I've ever been before, I always think, I'll go to New York first – then I'll kill myself. Now that I'm older and more idealistic, I know that going to the movies is better than death and New York City is one big movie show.

Maddie sighed. 'Religious holidays get on my nerves,' she said, staring down at the revellers in the park.

'You're sulking because the shops are shut.'

'I don't understand you. Why can't you come to L.A.? It's much nicer than New York. I promise I'll rent you a car.'

'Will we get invited to Pia Zadora's house?'

'Who?'

'Iggy Pop song.'

'What?'

'Never mind.'

I picked up the *Time Out* on her writing desk. *Mrs Parker* is on in the Prince Charles. I've seen it already in one of those French cinemas that used to be a church. It was playing to a half-empty house in Paris and I was annoyed with Alan Rudolph for having a beard in real life. His movies are seductive but I've never been able to talk myself into a man with a pog. To make matters worse, he bears a passing resemblance to Rumpelstiltskin. The powder dusting my nose and chin is irritating. I can feel it sitting in my pores. Bad mistake – using her puff.

'I think I'll go to a movie,' I said, acting casual.

'That's great,' she said. 'What am I supposed to do? The men aren't expected until seven.'

'Call the manicurist?' I suggested.

'You know full well I had everything done this morning. I'm perfect. All I need is a bath at six as a last-minute freshen up.'

'You can come with me if you like,' I said, confident. She hasn't been near a cinema since she picked up a flea at the Rio the year Marilyn Monroe died.

'I wouldn't dream of sitting in the black hole of Calcutta on a day like today,' she said. 'You want to watch it. One of these days you'll get murdered or something worse going to places like that by yourself.' I opened the door while she was still talking. That drives her barking. 'I pity the poor man who tries to rape you,' she called after me. 'You'd brain him!' Her harsh, smoky voice echoed along the corridor. 'Do you still have that wee gun I gave you?'

'You know it was stolen years ago,' I said, escaping round the corner.

As I waited for the lift, I half-expected her to catch up with me.

When the gun was stolen, I missed it. But my flat looked great empty. I bought a new bed and sat on it looking around at the mirror, television, video, telephone, make-up table, and CD player that replaced the lost items.

The gun was the only thing I missed and I couldn't replace it. Grandfather had stolen it when he was in the War. Maddie inherited it along with his other things. She gave it to me 'to defend myself' when a mad golfer shot an air pistol at us for stealing his balls.

Every Sunday we used to dress in emerald green and hide in the bushes at the edge of the course, darting out each time a ball came close. Later, we sold them half price in the Club House. Organized crime!

'Where did you get these?' the mad golfer demanded.

'We found them,' I said. The other golfers were happy with the buy-back no-questions-asked system. Some of them even profited in points when their opponents lost balls.

But the lunatic golfer persisted in keeping his eyes peeled. Rewarded, he caught me in the act – a daring run from the bushes to the seventh hole to bag not one but two balls. The following Sunday he was ready for me, air pistol loaded with pellets, but when he fired it was Vincent Tartellini – whose dad owned the chippie – who got shot in the bum. We ran home, John lugging the bag of golf balls, Vincent crying. And Vincent's dad slapped him before calling the doctor and giving me a big bag of deep-fried chips with a stinky pickled onion.

Maddie was outraged. 'You're not even eight years old,' she

169

kept saying, 'and you've just lost your grandfather.' She gave me the gun, saying, 'Don't hesitate: if you think someone's going to shoot at you — shoot first!'

After extracting a promise that we wouldn't use 'real bullets' (where would we get them?) but only the pellets and darts she provided, we dipped the darts in dog ka-ka to poison them for special occasions and set up a target in John's bedroom to shoot pellets at. Within days, we were crack shots and started charging money to any friend who failed to hit the bull's eye on entering or leaving.

The small well-proportioned marble lift with smoked-glass mirrors felt familiar as I descended to the Palm Court lobby. Mirrors remind me I'm being watched.

Silent couples sipping tea observed me as I made my way to the Arlington Street exit, accepting a sad smile from the Maître d' and a cheerful, 'Good afternoon!' from the slinky Chinese receptionist.

No princess today, going into Le Caprice. Celebrities keep themselves concealed on public holidays. Even an icon whose appeal is its ordinariness can't display this quality too often. Voyeurs have it all their own way, able always to watch some-body new; but the celeb is stuck in the same spotlight.

London was empty for the holiday as I walked to the chapel in Soho Square. Tourists in t-shirts wandered along Piccadilly, bewildered. You always underestimate the city you belong to. For years I hated it here, but now it's home. 'London is a white city,' Jack the New Yorker told me ages ago. New York is a scarlet city: sexy and scary and happening.

The heels of my new shoes felt like they were wearing down already. That happens to things that are brand new. Spoiled shoes and tooth decay are signs of mortality.

Dodging into a pharmacy with an Open All Day sign, I bought a small pair of scissors. The Red Rose bath oil also tempted me, but I didn't want to have to carry it. Anyway, I'd already stocked up on Ritz samples.

As I went into the deserted chapel, there was nobody behind me. Even after genuflecting, I kept looking back as I moved along the central aisle towards the altar. He is always watching me. At night he protects me, during the day he's willing me to join him. Particularly in a chapel, he's my audience, my reason for performance, my reminder of oblivion. We used to come here together to light white candles when he was in London for the day. He never spent the night in my flat but always travelled back after coming to see me. 'I don't like leaving my room alone too long,' he told me when I asked him to stay.

The last time I saw him, we didn't talk much after the first hour, just walked along happy in each other's presence. By the end of the day I was glad to get rid of him.

The scissors were burning a hole in my pocket. Out of the corner of my eye, as I released them from their smothering cellophane, I could see an old woman in black. Kneeling, rapt in chit-chat with God, she's a character from somebody else's movie. Concealed behind the altar, I crouched opening and closing my scissors to calm myself down. The last thing I need is the old bat to see me and come over to bless the souls of my unborn children. That happened to me three years ago in Barcelona. It's not an experience I'm eager to repeat. Old women are acceptable – so long as they're wearing gloves and don't try to paw you. Later on, this joint will be full of them on their knees for the Mass of the year.

We could have gone to the movies that day seven years ago

171

but there was nothing on we were desperate to see. We came here, unable to think of anything better. When we were wee, Maddie couldn't bear our piety.

'You're a pair of wee queer hawks,' she used to say. 'I should never have bought you those bibles. Your noses are never out of them.'

John was wearing his dark suit, very white shirt, boring shoes you could see your face in. I had on a scarlet cotton dress and flat pvc sandals.

John said, 'Jesus is the most uncool guy on the planet.' We were regarding a pink and blue crucifixion that didn't look like an antique. It's probably still here. Those paintings all look the same.

'God's dead glam,' I said.

'He has it,' John agreed, 'but not Jesus.'

'It's the pog,' I said, 'and the hair-do.'

'Yes,' John agreed. The conversation fizzled out. His fringe protected his eyes. Suddenly, there might have been tears on his lashes. But I couldn't be certain. Definitely wasn't planning to ask.

'When's your train?' Flying was one of the many things John didn't trust.

'Soon.' He kissed me on the lips, stood up, and walked out of the church.

At Euston Station, we had to run for it. He stopped halfway between the train and me, holding out his hand. 'Go on,' I shouted, breathless.

He waited, grabbing me, trying to drag me along for a proper goodbye on the platform. But I pulled away, stopped running, but continued following. He jumped on to the train, still extending his hand. The doors closed with perfect cinematic timing just as I caught up. He didn't have time to say it. The wounded look didn't really come into his eyes; I imagined it from memory.

No one
will
ever
love
you
like
I
do.

On the way back, I couldn't resist detouring into *Mrs Parker*. It had started already and I couldn't stay until the end so the fact that I appeared to be on the balcony alone probably doesn't count. John and me used to go up on the balcony in the Rio and throw popcorn and spit on the cineastes below, but only during rotten movies. If it was a *Carry On*, our eyes were glued to the screen, shoulders shaking.

What was the last movie we saw together? We didn't go to the cinema together much in London. The night we saw *New York, New York* with Debbie Harry he held my hand. It was exciting, knowing she was sitting behind us. It was before she was fat, but after she was dead famous. Nobody was going to mob her.

Why did I leave New York? I ran out of money. Maddie refused to send me more. She wanted me 'where she could see me', not in the city of drugs and murder. If there's one thing I know about myself, it's that I'm too frail to work for a living. I wasn't too proud to accept bits of my inheritance on the instalment plan. She didn't push her luck and insist on me going back to Glasgow. Little did she know, living in stinky King's Cross was more dangerously close to Hell than my hotel in midtown Manhattan.

It's great, having New York City there when you want it and need it. Like visiting your youth, or all the times you were ever happy. Last time I went there, the 8th Street cinema was dead. Posters for this and that pasted over its closed doors. New York never lets you down. It's imaginative enough to be Dorothy Parker's city and Martin Scorsese's at the same time. No matter how hot it gets, it never loses its beauty.

A wanker came in during Dottie's impulsive suicide attempt, and sat at the end of my row. The noise from the cut-throat, thumping, unseen from the camera was still in my ears as he unzipped his blue cotton trousers. The tiled New York bathroom is bathed in golden light, Dorothy wants to die, but knows she can't (yet) – but it's worth a try! She's the personification of twenties New York City and self-destructive glamour. And the wanker is panting and hissing.

'Excuse me,' I say, like I was taught when I was a Samaritan, 'are you masturbating?' Ninety-nine per cent of telephone wankers hang up when you ask that, but this guy was the one per cent.

'Yes,' he replied, 'and I'm enjoying it.' In the darkness, he looks a bit like Dr Grant – short and swarthy and intense.

'In here!' Maddie shouted from the bathroom. 'Where on earth have you been?' She's in the bath shrivelling her skin again. 'You'd better take a shower quick.'

'Not with you in here.'

'Don't be silly, I'm your mother.' A cigarette was smoking itself on the side of the tub, the toes of her old foot were resting on the gold taps. 'I've just had the one,' she said.

'I don't mind if you smoke yourself to death.'

'What else have I got? At my age! I've never been a drinker.'

176

'Apart from the medicinal brandy. And the champagne dinners. And the bedtime gin.'

'I hardly touch the stuff! Jon never uses alcohol. But I need my cigarettes. All these holidays make you fat.'

'No, make *you* fat. I can't afford holidays.'

My black Chanel cocktail dress was waiting for me on a hanger in the dressing room. I'd wanted to wear the bronze satin Prada dress, and Maddie had begged me to appear in the ridiculous pink thing she picked for me. We compromised with Coco.

On the video, she'd stuck a yellow Post It: Tape in the machine! She flounced in wearing a long white Ritz robe, like the one Charlie Castle wears in *The Big Knife*. Charlie's suicide is supposed to be noble and Roman, the only solution to avoid humiliation in Hollywood. But what sort of man slits his wrists in the bath when he's married to Ida Lupino? Her intelligent determined face alone is worth living for. Charlie wasn't protecting Marion with his death, he was deserting her. The courage it takes to make the lengthways slash into the vein, blue and tempting below that pure inner-arm skin, is cancelled by the lack of courage to go on living. And years later, Jack Palance played the villain in *Batman*. He didn't look like Charlie Cass any more. Ida probably still looks exactly like Marion, up there in Heaven with God and the rest of the gang.

'You look more like Grandfather Money every day,' I said. She sat at the mirror. 'Bathroom's free. By the way, I taped a film for you.'

I switched on the machine. 'Not now! You can take it away with you.'

'What is it?'

'One of the films you like. Can't remember the name – but

I knew it as soon as I saw it.' She ejected the tape and put it beside my other goodies.

'Right,' I said.

The shower's like Niagara Falls. During the inheritance tour, when we went on the *Maid of the Mist*, I refused to wear the red oilskin. The waterfall didn't look like it would drench me. But the boat sailed under, and I was soaked. She cackled under her mack, saying, 'You've had your comeuppance.'

But I like water. I love powerful showers. Baths are for wimps.

We were ready thirteen minutes early.

'What's the time?' I pointed at my Salvador Dali watch. 'I can't see that thing.'

'Look at your own.'

'I can't see with my contacts in.' Her unnaturally emerald eyes scan the room for a clock, alighting on a gold Louis-Seize ticking on the marble mantelpiece. 'What time is it on the clock?'

'Thirteen minutes to seven.'

'Is Dangerous punctual?' Is she talking too fast, or does she always talk fast?

'Yes.'

'Jon's always punctual.'

Silence.

'Should we wait up here or go downstairs?' she asked.

'Whatever you like.'

'What are you thinking about now?'

'Are you ever frightened?'

'What a question! That big brain of yours,' she sighed, 'and where did it get you? You,' she poked me in the kidney, her idea of affection, 'were always the cleverest in your class.'

'The other kids were dunderheads.'

'What's that supposed to mean? Don't forget I paid a fortune to have your I.Q. measured!' She disappeared into the dressing room, shouting, 'I just had a brilliant idea,' and came back wearing her Chanel dress. 'People will take us for sisters!' she shouted. 'You're my double now you're a blonde.'

We shared an insecure silence. In the background, I could hear French music.

'If you play your cards right,' Maddie said, 'you may get your hands on Jon's money as well.'

'Men his age usually have their own children – is he a shirt-lifter?'

'What a thing to say! He'll be here in a minute.' Affronted, but giggling, she asked, 'What's a shirt-lifter anyway? Knowing you, it must be something unpleasant.'

'I thought you didn't have any money left anyway.'

'I don't,' she said. When John died, I inherited his Kung Fu books. His will was a lipstick message on my mirror, *All my stuff is yours*. Maddie scrubbed it off, furious, smearing the Firebrand over the edges on to my white wall. 'What does he have to give away, tell me?' she kept repeating. 'Everything in that room of his was bought by me.'

She delved into her bag, pulling out an envelope. 'Before I forget,' she said, 'your birthday. I was going to give it to you tomorrow at the airport but I don't expect you'll be coming. I suppose that's why you don't have any children – you'd never be able to get them up in the morning.'

The white envelope contains a cheque for £7,000 dated 20th April.

'For a trip to New York or whatever you like,' she said. 'It's your birthday.' We could stay at the Algonquin. Even though it's an anglophile's paradise, a tourist trap, a ghost of its own past – I love that hotel! Since the *Mrs Parker* movie, sitting in the Blue Bar sipping champagne cocktails (even though Dorothy drank scotch) has been irresistible. Or we could go to the Plaza, where Irene the Slut was trapped in the elevator with Steve McQueen. 'My only regret,' Auntie Irene told Maddie when she called her long distance to boast, 'is that it wasn't Paul Newman.'

'Thanks, Mum.' I never call her that, only Maddie.

'Buy yourself something nice,' she said, sticking out her cheek for a kiss – determined to extract her pound of flab. 'But be on your best behaviour tonight. Don't say anything weird to Jon. And don't forget that tape, after me going to the trouble of recording it for you.' She stooped to pick up the video, shoved it into one of my bags, pleased with herself. 'Just wait till your husband sees everything I've bought you! Though I think you should have worn the pink tonight. Surprised everybody. Instead of looking like you're on your way to a wake all the time.'

I looked at the time. Seven minutes past seven. After today, I'm safe. Some people have to go around gloom-ballooning every day. My turn only comes up once a year. I'm lucky, lucky.

A Place in the Sun

'Your mum's not a bad old bore,' Dangerous said, as we walked up Bond Street loaded down with my packages but delaying the moment when we'd stop a taxi, after escaping from her and the surprisingly elegant Jon. 'She must have ordered at least seven bottles of champagne.'

'She drinks faster when she's nervous.'

'She wasn't even drunk!'

'Years of practice,' I said, glancing at the empty Cartier window. During the day, tiaras nobody buys adorn the small serene jeweller's shops, familiar from snatch-and-grab movies. Grinning green, mad ruby, and mysterious sapphire stones competing with each other in a world where diamonds are still a blonde's first choice.

'And that Jon! I was expecting a fat turd in checked pants. His suit was great. He looks like Tommy Newton in *The Man Who Fell to Earth*.'

'Tommy Newton in the book or David Bowie in the film?'

'A cross between the two.' Jon's thin, with the cheekbones; silent rather than shy; astonishingly likeable, with a keep-out barrier circling him. Deep and strange and far away, as Elizabeth says to Monty. God knows what Jon the millionaire sees in

Maddie. That woman certainly has a knack for attracting money.

'And he insisted on paying the bill after all those oysters you gulped. What a guy!' We collapsed laughing on the pavement. 'Should we smash a window?' Dangerous asked. Unprovoked violence (so long as there's no blood) is just the touch to top off an entertaining evening – and I'd actually enjoyed myself!

'Of course I see what you mean about her being a nutter,' Dangerous said. 'What was all that business about the book?'

I'd given Maddie the new kiss & smell Elizabeth Taylor biog to read on the plane home. 'Oh goodie,' she said, 'a book. Maria will have warned you – I actually read books. Or do you call her Carole? Very pious when she was young you know. Never off her knees – and I was the one who had to wash the white stockings.' Maddie's never done a hand-washing in her life. She used to give all our whites to Grandfather's battleaxe girlfriend, Gorm, who has a passion for soap powder.

'Irene the Slut's Chinese boyfriend gave her three books for Christmas.'

'One of her sisters?'

'The one she hates the most.'

'What's Irene the Slut's Christmas present got to do with Liz Taylor?'

'Nothing. Irene the Slut used one of her books to balance the wobble in the leg of her dressing table, one to make herself bigger in the driver's seat in the car that killed her, and one was kept in her handbag to give it extra clonking power.'

'Did she read the books first?'

'Of course not. They were Chinese. But the really shameful thing – Maddie used to say to me when I was wee and she told me this story at bedtime – is that the books were secondhand! He didn't even think enough of her to buy them brand new in Barnes & Noble.'

182

One night, I asked sleepily, 'Will Auntie Irene come with us to Barnes & Noble when we go to New York?'

'Of course not,' Maddie said. 'Irene's dead.'

'Oh yes, I forgot.'

'And thank God for that, otherwise we'd have ended up treating her in the Russian Tea Room.' Her sisters never have any money. Maddie looks down on people who don't have a huge disposable income.

Dangerous Sieg Heil'd a taxi outside Loewe's. As it screeched to a halt, he asked, 'Did anything happen between you and your brother?'

'What you mean the incest?' I replied, climbing in first. In the dark of the back seat, his face is curious, serious, alarmed. Nobody says anything. The driver's listening. Our silence is too definite.

As the cab spun round Marble Arch, he held my hand. Driving in the dark doesn't terrify me the way driving in daylight does. Going up Edgware Road, we passed chatterbugging Arabs sitting outside drinking coffee. They don't give a fuck about Easter or caffeine-induced insomnia.

While Dangerous was paying the cab, I stood counting stars. 'Seven stars, a good omen,' I told him as he walked towards me, smiling.

'Did you love him?' he asked as we went inside. Fishface, the man upstairs, suddenly appeared behind us. The three of us waited for the lift.

'There's no answer to that,' I said to Dangerous. Fishface stared straight ahead.

The lift stopped on the first floor and Rachel the Irish waitress got in. At night, she doubles up as the porter's wife. 'My God,' she said, 'your hair! I've just been delivering a snack to the old beast. She never remembers to eat on a bank holiday. Too bad I don't have that problem! I'll swing for that Old Anna one of these days – says she doesn't like cheese! Bloody cheek. She ate a lasagne the other day in the kaff.' When I see Old Anna at Mass I pretend not to recognize her in case she kneels beside me, giving me a free whiff of under-arm odour.

'You love her really,' I said.

'I can't get over you as a blonde,' Rachel said, getting out at her floor.

Once we were in our flat, Dangerous persisted, 'You mean you did?'

'I mean I don't,' I replied, putting a record on. Records are fragile and tactile, their mortality makes them more intense than CDs. 'He's only interesting because he's dead. He did it on purpose.'

'Well,' he said, pushing his natural blond hair out of his eyes. 'Shall we watch that video Maddie gave you, or have a dance?'

'Definitely a dance,' I said, kicking my shoes off. 'She always cuts the end off a film.' Serge Gainsbourg's singing, *Incest is a crime. The love you will never know together is Heaven sent.* Then again, my French has never been that good.

'What is it anyway?'

'I don't know.' He knows when I'm lying. I haven't looked, but I know she's taped *A Place in the Sun.* It was on again yesterday.

'What are you thinking?' Heaven. Hell. Hollywood. He can read my mind, he just wants to see if I'll admit it.

'Holidays in New York!'

'New York, New York,' he shouted, spinning me round. Breathless, he said, 'We could always go to L.A. too if you like.'

184

'I'd be disappointed.' He didn't say anything. 'I hate traffic.' The music was making us drunk. 'The flight's too long.' I can feel his heart, thudding. 'It'll be sunny.' Dangerous smiled without replying, the correct way to treat a wife who's repeating her old excuses.

'Is madness hereditary?'

'You're frighteningly sane.'

When Eva Marie Saint visits the *On the Waterfront* roof wearing her Mary Magdalene nightgown, she accidentally on purpose meets Marlon Brando for a kiss. Their audience is silent and unseen.

When Dangerous fell asleep, I put on more lipstick to liven myself up, took a cold bottle of water out of the fridge and climbed the stairs to the roof.

Ascending, I'm aware of John's eyes on my back. If I stop being convinced there's an audience, I'm dead. It's easy to believe this when you've grown up glued to the screen, one of a generation of voyeurs watching for a reflection.

Loads of lights are still on. Standing at the edge, I can smell the garden below and see its solemn shape carved into the insides of the building. Bits of sofas and vases of yellow roses are reflected into it by the bedside lamps of insomniacs. Opposite, I can see someone watching television. Impossible to tell what he's tuned into. I could be downstairs watching *A Place in the Sun*. But I've seen it before.

Last time I came up here Irish Rachel and the porter were entertaining her sister from Dublin who was in London looking for a man. Their deck chairs are lolling, empty, in the half-light. I wouldn't dream of sitting down. Having a wee chat with God only works standing up with a view of the stars. God isn't Cary Grant any more. Tonight He looks more like Maddie, sitting with her feet in a basin of water, writing instructions on the back of a cheque: *To be spent on a HOLIDAY*. As she reminded me again tonight, 'I'm closer to death than birth now.' She looks more like Grandfather Money every time I see her.

God must be bored sick watching everything all the time, listening to grovelling Christians or sourpusses complaining that He doesn't exist.

Omnipotence would be great fun if it didn't come in a package with omniscience and omnipresence.

Telling people your dreams usually bores them to tears, especially first thing in the morning. Confessing your prayers would allow a little bit of your soul to be stolen.

I've always wanted to be brave. For years fear has been following me. I didn't love John enough. I didn't want to save him. The love that was never meant is Heaven sent. There are some things that break your heart especially when they're not intended to. Ice cream melting in the darkness. Rust suddenly appearing on your favourite scissors. Realizing you didn't love someone you've been pretending to love your whole life. Not loving someone enough is the same as not loving them. Love can't exist unless it means everything.

I couldn't love Dangerous more.

My flesh and my blood. My soul. The most potent. The purest sense. The most intense.

Standing there, time flew – the way it does when you're happy. The stars died. It isn't John's big day any more. I've passed the significant seventh year. My dead glam loss is something I'll always have, to nurture in dark days, but that broken mirror I smashed because they were burning my brother can't hurt me now.

Next Easter he'll die again. And the year after that. He'll go on and on dying every year before my birthday. And I'll be resurrected.

Opening the door at sunrise, I tiptoed across the white carpet, holding my breath. But Dangerous was up already, scooping coffee from the freezer into the percolator.

He said, 'Let's go to the airport and wave her off.'

The End

Airports are obvious death metaphors. Apart from all the excitement of terrorism, the literal ascent into the sky is a reminder of the spirit rising to Heaven – or the inevitable fear of crashing.

When someone famous dies, in a plane crash or from a disease or – feebly – while asleep, it's automatically a 'tragedy' whether anyone will be heartbroken or not. When a large group of people are killed accidentally it's a 'catastrophe' even though they may all have been bastards, and God's got to keep an eye on population control, and everybody dies some time.

Suicide is a way of controlling death. It's the big fuck off, the death that's unanswerable. The suicide has the last word, leaving the living repulsed, envious and fascinated.

The plane climbs above the clouds, closer to Heaven. Dangerous holds my hand, though I've never been afraid of flying. He likes touching me.

'Your skin's cold,' he says, 'like your brave little heart.'

The stewardess is serving pink champagne. Even the businessmen are smiling. Visiting Hollywood is like meeting your hero, if you're still pure enough to have one. There's also a perverse – or positive – pleasure in destroying a dream.

Going on living is a compromise unless you're happy. Happiness is the key to eternal life. You have to be really brave to be happy.

'What are you smiling at?' Dangerous asks.

'We're going to the land where movies weren't invented.'

'You'd better be careful of all that happiness,' he says, imitating Maddie. He's an excellent actor. But he's too clever to be an actor. He's dead glamorous, but doesn't have a self-destructive bone in his body. My hero's a thrill a minute, and he has blond hair.